Christine Brendle

A Cottage in Maine

When Winter came

Novel

C. M. Brendle Verlag

Impressum:

C. M. Brendle Verlag

Copyright © 2020 by Christine Brendle

First Published in Germany 2018

Cover: C. M. Brendle Verlag

Translated from German

Johanna Ellsworth

ISBN: 978-3-942796-33-0

www.brendle-verlag.de

1

The suitcases are packed; everything is ready for my departure. Once again I walk through the house, although I don't think I've forgotten anything. Maybe I just need those few minutes. Sunlight floods the room in the attic. The Boston sky is blue, blue and clear. As clear as my decision. I'm sure about that at least, though about nothing else. What a view, the most beautiful one from anywhere in the house. Like a glittering ribbon, the Charles River flows wide and slow far below me. My study. Here I wanted to write my novel. I never got beyond the first few pages. A leaden paralysis prevented me from writing. It wasn't because of this room. A deep depression overcame me at a time that was meant to be my happiest. I had made a terrible mistake.

I close the window. The room looks empty without the computer and printer. In the baskets on the empty desk there are some sheets of paper. Notes on my novel, flashes of thought that proved worthless the moment I wanted to put them on paper. At the bottom there is a note with window measurements for curtain poles and fabric. It dates back to the very beginning, when I had new curtains sewn for the bedroom and bathroom. I had bought plants and placed them all over the house. All my attempts were in vain; Dan's house never became my home.

I tear the sheets into small snippets and throw them in the trash. My bed in the bedroom is made as if I were leaving for just a few days. I also left the bathroom unchanged. My toothbrush is still in its usual place, and so is the perfume I last used. Until the end I didn't have the courage to tell Dan the whole truth. He is waiting for me at the bottom of the stairs. The luggage has disappeared from the hallway. Dan is breathing heavily.

»Is that all, Karen?«

»Yes, that's all. Thank you, Dan.«

»Well, it's about all that fits in the car.«

»Then I'll carry Leo in his basket.«

My young tomcat lies in his basket, sleeping. When I pick him up, he barely stirs. The sedative drops I gave him are already working. I gently put him into the travel box and close the lid.

»If you'd at least leave him here, I'd know that you'll be back soon.«

»Then he'd be alone with you all day.«

»Sometimes I think you love him more than me.«

»But you gave him to me.«

»To cheer you up.«

»He has often done a good job of cheering me up.«

»Karen, you can still change your mind.«

»Now?«

»It's really simple: Just call and say you've changed your mind.«

»But I haven't change my mind, Dan.«

»We could do things differently; we could travel more often ...«

»Let's not start again.«

Dan looks more helpless than I've ever seen him.

»I'll miss you. Will you miss me, too?« Tears glitter in his eyes. Suddenly he embraces me. »Won't you give us a chance?«

I feel as if a web is spinning around me, denser and denser. It turns into a solid cocoon, making me rigid and motionless.

»Let me go, please, let me go.«

He clasps my hand. I start to feel annoyed.

»You can't wait to get away.«

Suddenly I feel guilty. Living together was our dream.

»Dan, it's not easy for me either.«

Finally he lets me go.

»Okay. Will you get in touch with me?«

»Yes, but give me time.«

I kiss him on the cheek, take the basket with the cat, turn around and walk out the front door, hurrying down the few steps, through the small front yard, along the footpath to the parking lot, where the packed car is waiting. Dan follows me. Time, I need time. I'm glad when I finally sit in the car and step on the gas. I catch only a brief glimpse of Dan in the rearview mirror. Then everything runs its course. I'm on the road. No one can stop me anymore. And I can't change my mind anymore.

2

The city is jammed with traffic. It's just before nine a.m., commuter traffic. The required concentration distracts me. Behind Boston things are getting quieter. It is the 28th of August, the summer holidays will be over soon. In the opposite lane, the vacationers are returning from Maine. There is little traffic going in my direction. I'm driving against the current, and on the highway that is finally an advantage. Trees fly past me, seagulls. Or am *I* flying? The Atlantic flashes dark blue through houses and bushes. I am leaving everything behind. Dan, Rita, Robert, my parents' calls and letters, their disappointment. They would have loved to see me become a wife and mother. A dream so tangible – and now so abruptly destroyed. A family life that also corresponded to my idea of a perfect life: my mother, how pretty she always was, with her short brown hair, and how happy at my father's side. And Dad, my beloved dad, always calm and friendly, shaped my image of a perfect husband. My grandmother was happy in her marriage, too. Although her first husband had passed away too soon, »Grandfather Paul« had filled the gap he had left perfectly. Happy women, for generations. Suddenly I would see them everywhere: young wives and mothers, content, pleasant, patent, complacent, with rosy-cheeked angels in strollers or holding hands. It seemed to be the most natural thing in the world. Only I was obviously completely unsuitable for this. These thoughts upset me. I turn on the radio. Music blares. Pop music, cheerful and light, just the right music for this late summer day, blue and carefree, as if this summer had only just begun, not as if it were already coming to an end.

Surprisingly quick I've reached Portland, then Yarmouth, Freeport, Brunswick and Bath. At the Intown Pub I can pick up the key. Grace is busy behind the counter. The pub is crowded; it's lunch time. She only spots me when I am right in front of her.

»Oh, you're already here? I didn't expect you so early.«

»Yes, there was little traffic on the highway. I thought there wouldn't be anybody in Maine anymore.«

»Well, as you can see, there are still enough people around. However, there're not that many tourists here, rather the people who live here. Why don't you take a seat. Would you like something to eat?«

After a quick look at the crowded room I decide to drive on. Grace is pleasant, just like she was last spring, yet I feel strangely shy around her.

»I'll better just drive on; my cat is in the car. I gave him a sedative but he'll probably wake up soon and get upset.«

Grace seems a little surprised but she doesn't urge me to stay.

»Will you find the way?«

»Yes, I think so.«

She briefly tells me how to get to 209. »You can take it to Popham Beach. Take a right turn shortly after the entrance to the national park.«

I almost miss the turn-off. The narrow path has grown over with weeds during the summer. At the last minute I turn the steering wheel and enter the green thicket. The car slowly rolls on. The thick foliage slaps against its sides. Shortly after, the wall of leaves opens up and everything is as I remember it. The endless surface of the Atlantic gently rocking in front of me. There is no one on the beach. The small inconspicuous wooden cottage, nestling close to the forest and facing the sea, looks as if it is sleeping with closed shutters. I drive up to the steps that lead to the front door behind its small wooden patio. Nothing moves in the basket on the passenger seat. Oh my God, what if the sedative was too strong? Panicking, I open the grid and shake the tiger-striped fur ball. Leo moves but he doesn't wake up. At least he's still alive.

It is dark in the house, and I am greeted by hot air. The smell is familiar. It smells like my grandparents' cottage on Lake Michigan. Almost instantly I feel at home. I open the shutters to air out the room. I hardly remember the rooms except the living room with its dark wood and leather furniture. The dimly lit kitchen that faces the forest comes with the most necessary equipment: a stove, a fridge, a cupboard for food and dishes, and a sink by the window. In the center of the room there is a dark wooden table with four chairs. An envelope with the words For Karen in large, sweeping letters sits on the table. The letter is from Clifford. He wishes me a nice stay.

… If you have any questions, please contact Grace. She has been looking after the house in my absence for years and knows everything there is to know about the house. She is also a fantastic counselor.

Perhaps I will also get the chance to stop by myself. I would like to see our discussion from spring continued.

Best regards, Clifford

He thinks a lot about Grace, as I noticed back in May, when he urged me to go to her restaurant for lunch after the interview. She supposedly serves the juiciest steaks and biggest hamburgers. The two of them seem to have been friends for many years. Were they once a couple? But in the next moment this idea seems absurd. They are too different. Clifford has a strong personality, is cheerful and easygoing, while Grace seems so sober and austere. Does she think of me as Clifford's friend? Or what reason did he give her for my staying in his house for the next months?

3

The rooms are meticulously clean. Nothing reminds me of the fact that Clifford lived here until just a few days ago. Did he take everything with him? Or was it Grace? It would suit her. I check the cupboards. Thank God, there are enough pots and dishes. I didn't see the upper floor when I last visited the house. Now I realize that a single large room with built-in closets and a bed in the center takes up almost the whole space. In addition, there is only a tiny bathroom, which was probably once built into bedroom. It features an old-fashioned white claw-foot bathtub. A white pla-stic curtain is draped around it so it can also be used as a shower. The ceramic sink is modern and quite large, as is the mirror on the wall. My face looks pale in the glaring sunlight, and my hair, which is tinted red, reinforces that impression. I discover a few tiny wrinkles. My God, I look old! Am I getting old at the age of thirty-five or did I really age that much in the last year? I never thought about getting older. Why should I? Just a year ago I believed that my real life was just beginning. But what is that, a real life?

I turn away from the mirror and go back downstairs. In the kitchen I turn on the old-fashioned coffee maker and sincerely hope it won't explode. The peaceful gurgling sound calms me down, and I start taking my luggage out of the car. While I am putting the noodle and rice packages away, I finally hear a soft mewing coming from the basket. Relieved I open the screen grid. Leo looks a bit sleepy but otherwise okay. I pet him and talk to him in a soothing voice. He sniffs my hand and climbs awkwardly out of the box. Looking astonished, he takes a few stiff steps. I fill up his food bowl, but he just sniffs at it, turns around and walks curiously towards the living room. I follow him. The new environment and the unfamiliar smells seem to fascinate him. Looking through the window, I can see a few people walking on the beach.

It's almost four. I pour coffee into the largest cup I can find and walk outside to the patio with it. Leo wants to follow me, but a gust of wind makes him pull back. My spoiled cat has never been exposed to wind before. His puzzled face makes me laugh.

»Get used to the house first, there are plenty of new things for you to explore inside.« The door swings shut.

I sit down on the weathered wooden bench. In the same spot I sat in May of this year. It was only a short stay but it brought about a lot of changes. It was just a small job, but it was my first reportage as a freelancer for Globus. Until autumn of last year I had traveled almost all over the world as a salaried employee of the travel magazine publisher. After eight months of abstinence and a monotonous existence as a housewife the small job seemed like a lifeline. It had probably saved me at the last moment from sinking into lethargy and depression for good. A new amusement park had opened in Maine - with a fun pool, fitness rooms, saunas and solariums - as they have mushroomed in all parts of the country lately. I was to present it and the immediate surrounding region to the readers. The swimming pool turned out to be hardly spectacular, but the landscape enchanted me all the more.

I was fascinated by the rugged coastline with its picturesque harbors and lighthouses, the immensity of the maple forests, the charm of the frequently nostalgic, cozy towns. The lobsters tasted more delicious here than anywhere else in the world. I met Clifford towards the end of my stay. The actor of the Brunswick Music Theater was preparing for his 25th summer season. After eating at the pub, he invited me to his house on Popham Beach.

»You can't possibly go back to Boston without getting to know my beach. If you haven't seen it, you don't know the area,« he claimed.

The long sandy beach, which is unusually flat for the region, really amazed me. The cozy wooden cottage had a homely atmosphere, and the view from the terrace made me exclaim enthusiastically: »What a wonderful place! I could write here!«

Then I told him about my novel, which I hadn't touched in months, and Clifford suggested, »Why don't you come here? I work in New York from September to April, and the house is vacant during that time. I'd be happy if you stayed here. This landscape is full of magic; it's perfect for artists.«

At the time I had refused to take him up on his offer, laughing it off, but the idea stayed on my mind. It sat in the back of my head, growing day by day until I couldn't think anymore of anything else. I envisioned what it would be like to just get in the car and drive off. I wouldn't have to explain anything to anyone, I'd just go away, and no one would know where I was. I could write the story in the mornings and in the evenings, relax between long walks, and a few months later I would resurface with the finished manuscript. And in the meantime all my other problems would have disappear into thin air.

After returning from Maine, the days in Boston became even more unbearable. So one day I called Clifford and accepted his offer.

Sun rays tickle my face. I relax and close my eyes. The gentle breeze strokes my skin. Now it is rush hour in Boston. Countless cars are clogging the streets; the air is filled with noise and pollution. How infinitely far away all this seems to be. Much further away than just a three-hour drive. All of a sudden it gets chilly out here. The sun is gone; it is getting dark. There is no one on the beach anymore. The Atlantic gleams mysteriously; it looks like dark-blue ink. I'm wrapped in silence. Shivering, I step inside. Leo welcomes me happily. I pick him up and bury my face in his fur.

I spend half the night moving furniture and putting my things into closets while drinking the heavy red wine Dan gave me as a farewell present. At some point the day breaks away from time. What was that? A thump startles me. Suddenly the room is filled with bright light. Blinded, I close my eyes and sink back into the pillows.

»What do you want, Leo? It's still too early.« With closed eyes I stroke his fur. I feel shattered. I can hear the sound of the waves and the screams of the seagulls outside. The last shreds of my dream fade in the bright daylight. I had gotten lost in the traffic chaos of a foreign city. At some point I lost my shoes and purse. I waved at the passing cabs but none of them stopped. Barefoot, I ran back to all the places where I had been. Many abandoned purses and shoes were shown to me; mine were not among them. Yet many people seemed to have lost their purses and shoes.

I am relieved when I realize where I am. My goodness, it's already ten - late in the morning! When did I go to bed? Did I have too much wine? I pad downstairs. The large living room table with the computers and printers on it is in front of the window. My workplace is ready, including the neat piles of paper. The wine bottle in the kitchen is empty. What I need first now is coffee. Then I change my mind. Still dressed in my bathrobe, I walk the few yards down to the deserted beach. Spontaneously I drop my bathrobe and run into the water. The cold water takes my breath away, but after a few strokes I am awake. When I leave the water a few minutes later, a cold breeze sinks its sharp teeth into my wet skin. I wrap myself into my bathrobe and hurry back to the house. Leo greets me loudly.

»Are you hungry?« Once again I fill his bowl, and this time he starts to eat greedily. I turn the coffeemaker on and take a shower. The hot water is steaming and my body starts to glow as if pricked with fine needles. After my shower I feel better.

4

After a quick breakfast I sit down at my desk. For the first time in months, I open the blue folder. I can hardly remember what I have written. I peruse the pages. What I read is not exactly thrilling. My main characters, Sarah and Tom, are colorless and shapeless. The whole story is a bone-dry skeleton. I remember my countless attempts to make it lively. But the sentences and words come along as if they were walking on stilts, the text seems to rebel against me. I start to get doubts. Is there something wrong with the story?

My gaze wanders outside. A red kite flutters in the sky, climbing higher and higher; it sways, seems to float, then it suddenly races along the beach and starts to tremble, tugging at an invisible string. I wish the string would break and it would fly away into the infinite blue.

I need to exercise anyway. So I close the folder and go to the beach. Soon I find myself in the middle of a happy crowd. The beautiful weather has drawn many people to the beach. Seagulls circle in one spot. Somebody is feeding them. Screeching, they swoop down to the morsels that are thrown at them. The red kite tugs at its string; a man tries to tame it while running. His two children stumble after him, squealing. I seem to be the only person without company. Suddenly I feel like a foreign body in this cheerful setting. I wander through the crowd, nearly bumping into a girl. A young man who follows her tries to grab her.

»Excuse me!« The girl giggles exuberantly behind my back. I walk faster. Suddenly the crowd becomes unbearable. I start to feel better when the voices become more distant and I have finally left them behind. Now all I hear is the sound of the waves. »Tourists are rare in the fall,« Clifford had said. Actually I prefer it that way. Maybe that was one of the main reasons why I came here. The road ends unexpectedly. It is blocked by a high cliff and water worn stones. I did not realize how far I've walked. I can't see the other beach goers anymore. My hands are filled with shells I collected on the way. It is a passion I cannot resist whenever I am at the beach. Like most people, I'm fascinated by these beautiful filigree shapes, which are really just the shells of living creatures I hardly know anything about. Is it because they come from the depths of the sea, from where we humans originally came from, too? Or does our fascination come from their ability to form pearls in response to the invasion of foreign bodies? I don't know. I sit down on one of the smaller rocks, put the shells into the sand next to me, forming them into a pattern. All that remains is the crashing of the waves and the smacking sound they make between the stones. At that moment I feel like a shell washed ashore. Somewhere there, far behind the horizon, is Europe. Paris, London, Berlin, Madrid, and Rome. My first trip for Globus had taken me to Rome.

Suddenly I am flooded with sadness. I fell in love with Rome the minute I laid eyes on it. Like an enchanted child I ran run through that vibrant city. At night I could hardly sleep; I would lie awake for hours in the small hotel right in the center, listening to the rattling of mopeds and the seemingly never-ending murmur of voices until dawn. I'd love to write about Rome, I suddenly think. Why doesn't my story play in Rome? Sarah, a young American, visits this city for the first time. I see her in the narrow room with the endlessly high ceiling and the old dark furniture. I can envision her on the Spanish Steps and at the Colosseum, the Roman Forum and the Trevi Fountain. Tom would not be called Tom but Ricardo or Roberto. It could be a love story. A gentle story, a bit touching and wonderfully romantic. Roma, a city whose name, spelled backwards, already contains the word for love: amor. Cupid. Which city would be better suited for a love story?

Stop. I have to stop. Me and a love story… The idea seems absurd. I remember the series of unfortunate love stories in recent years. Most recently the abrupt end of my relationship with a colleague of mine at the Salem Post, which was why I quit my job and went to Globus. Rita, my co-worker and best friend, couldn't understand it. It made her sad and angry at the same time.

»And just because of a man! If I changed my job every time I broke up with some guy, I wouldn't stay anywhere for more than four weeks.«

She was right, and yet ... Rita was different from me. She fell in love all the time. As fast as the men showed up in her life, they would disappear again. Then Rita would sob miserably on her bed or mine for hours, swearing that she'd never fall in love again. But while I was still mad at the man who had made my friend so miserable, she would happily return with that telltale silky gloss in her eyes. She had just met the man of her dreams. Rita was a phenomenon. I, on the other hand, had decided to focus only on my job.

I wanted to travel, get to know the world and have a successful career. Two years later, Dan came across my way – or rather my plate. It was in Boston, at the opening of a new office wing of Globus. At the cold buffet I bumped right into him with my salad plate. Whereupon white salad dressing trickled in small rivulets over his dark blue jacket, and green endive lettuce curled on his tie. A few inches further up I looked into a pair of blue eyes that smiled in amusement. My helpless attempt to remove the stains with hot water from the tea kitchen were answered by his spontaneous invitation to the Margarita, the restaurant on the rooftop where he could eat without wearing a jacket.

It turned out that the handsome blonde man was one of the architects who planned the new part of the building. Something I had no longer believed could happen did happen. The man I fell in love with this time was single and faithful. For two years we were happy. I had felt safe with him and loved him until I made that fateful decision.

Two years after we met I gave in to Dan's pleas – I quit my job and moved in with him. Everything changed after that. I don't know the specific day or exact hour when our love left us. It just walked away, quiet and unnoticed, and eventually became a heavy word without any meaning.

I collect my shells and make my way back. The crowd on the beach has become even denser. Nevertheless, I recognize some of the faces. The scenery has changed only little. The red kite lies defeated on the ground. The two children are building sandcastles. The young lovers are peacefully dozing next to each other in the sand. Their faces look even younger, almost childlike. What do you dream and what will come true for you?

No, I won't write a love story. There will be no Ricardo or Roberto. I will write about the world and the life I know.

5

I heat up a can of ravioli in the kitchen, and as I stir the pasta in the pot, I can suddenly envision them clearly: Sarah and Tom. They have young faces that are still blank, like white sheets of paper. They resemble the lovers on the beach. And now I know: I would like to start out with them. I will watch them laugh, love and live. I feel a sense of adventure inside me. It's as if I was on a journey to a faraway unknown land. At the same time I suspect I will discover things that are important for my own life.

A new daily rhythm starts almost by itself. I get up early and go to bed early. After getting up, I swim; then I work for several hours. Then I take a long walk. I quickly get used to my little house. The smell of wood, water and sand reminds me of my childhood vacations in the log cabin on Lake Michigan. Its voices are also familiar to me, the creaking and crackling in the timbers or the sighing when the wind sweeps around its corners. Every day it is a bit more my home. Small shell arrangements soon decorate all the shelves and window sills, and grasses and branches are scattered in vases all over the cottage. At the same time, the house is subject to constant change, as I am, too. My unrest gives way to a velvety calmness and serenity.

Leo has become accustomed to our new domicile. My playful kitty has become an enthusiastic stray. After a few cautious explorations he is soon on the move for ever longer periods of time. The pine forest behind the house has become his favorite territory. It doesn't take long before he proudly presents me with his first prey: a large, freshly killed mouse that is still warm. The tiny ball of fur Dan conjured out of his jacket a few months ago has turned into a big adult cat. He is obviously happy, and I can hardly imagine that he will ever get use to the crowded life in a city apartment. For the time being I push this idea into the farthest corner of my heart.

I'm making good progress with my story. Tom and Sarah work as tour guides in the exclusive resort of an American tour operator in Sri Lanka. It is the couple's first joint mission so far away from home. The surroundings, the exotic park around the hotel and its seafront location make Tom very happy. Sarah, who is usually the active one and driving force, however, is having a hard time. The petite blonde suffers from the hot and humid weather. She even has her problems with the cheerful colleagues, who talk and happily giggle all the time. She finds them to be superficial. Tom loves his new work. Popular with guests and colleagues alike, he soon takes over the day trips.

Sarah feels hurt by Tom's enthusiasm. It feels like a betrayal to her. How can he be so happy while she feels so miserable? She is irritated. Dark clouds taint their relationship. And then Shirley, the new girl, a spirited Brazilian, turns up. Sarah hates her from the start.

I've lost weight. I can tell by my suddenly baggy jeans. My face has become leaner, too. Or is it because my hair has grown and is already touching my shoulders? A suntanned face greets me in the mirror; my skin glows, as I see with satisfaction. I drive to Bath once a week to do my laundry in the small laundromat on Mainstreet; afterwards I go shopping. My shopping lists have become simple: food, toothpaste, soap, skin cream. I barely use cosmetics or even perfume anymore. I'm no longer interested in fashion;, I'm only wearing jeans anyway. When I am done with shopping, I stop by at the Intown Pub. I've started to like Grace. I realize she's not rude, just so different from all the women I've ever met before. She fits in here, reminding me of Maine's brittle, restrained stillness and cool clarity.

We've become friends. Grace collects my mail. Mostly it is letters from Mom, who worries about me.

The more she complains, the more it confirms my feeling that it was right not to get a phone. This way my little house on the beach is my island where nobody bothers me.

At Grace's I read the papers, eat something and hear the latest news about this area. The daughter of Mr. Jones, the owner of Bradberry Store, married her long-time fiancé; they had a glamorous wedding. Mrs. Jonathan Dalton, who had committed her life to Pinetree Hill, the local retirement home, passed away at the age of 89, and the Passaro family was visited by their niece from Europe. My world has become small. From Grace's pub I call Dan. His voice sounds depressed. No, he doesn't blame me for what happened, and yet I feel guilty. Every time I call him I feel more down than before. Although he doesn't say it, I know he is miserable and hopes that I'll return to Boston soon, while, emotionally, I move farther away from him each day. Grace is aware of it. After the phone call she gently touches my shoulder and says, »Oh yeah, these tough guys. Don't take it too hard, girl. He'll get over it.«

In fact, it is precisely her sober, pragmatic way that helps me most in moments like these. In my novel, the crisis is coming to a head. I have increased my workload. The tension is tangible. Shirley, the spirited Brazilian, whirls around the sleepy resort like a hurricane. Sarah is feeling worse. Her feminine instincts signal that there is danger ahead. Distressed, she befriends her female co-workers. The team behaves like a startled beehive. The women whisper and speculate. Stories make the rounds. »She comes from a poor family. She picks up guys, seduces them, and then she sends them away.« They condemn Shirley and at the same time envy her. The guests like her. The men look at her. Shirley herself doesn't seem to notice any of this. Unconcerned and happy, she animates the guests to do idiosyncratic morning gymnastics, organizes sandcastle building competitions for the children and obstacle courses for young people. She overcomes all hurdles like a lithe cat, swims like a dolphin in the pool. In the evenings, she dances tango with Ricardo, her Argentine counterpart, on the small dance floor of the bar. Guests and her co-workers watch the couple, entranced.

She's so natural and straightforward, Tom thinks. She's a witch, Sarah hisses mentally.

»Hey, I'm still here, too,« she says sharply.

»What's that supposed to mean? I know you're here.«

»Oh really? You've had nothing but eyes for her for the past thirty minutes!«

»You're exaggerating. They've only been dancing for five minutes.«

»She's already wraping you around her little finger, haven't you noticed?«

»Sarah, why are you saying that? Your moods are driving me crazy.«

»I drive you crazy? No, my dear, she's driving you crazy.«

»Have you gone totally nuts?«

Sarah knows that her accusations are making things only worse but she cannot help it. She can't stop causing ever more violent scenes. The more Sarah complains about Shirley, the more Tom thinks he has to defend her. The more he defends her, the more excited Sarah gets. I follow the development almost breathlessly. Tom starts to compare the two women. At first sight, Sarah, now almost platin-blonde from the sun, and Shirley, black-haired with a dark complexion, are as different as day and night. Shirley has a very feminine figure while Sarah looks almost haggard.

Their tempers are even more different. I can clearly envision the women me: Sarah with her defiant, hurt expression, sad blue eyes and narrow, tightly pressed lips. In comparison to her Shirley's eyes are almost provocative. Her full lips smile knowingly when she is not talking gaily. Tom is fascinated by Shirley's dark voice and her temperament. Is Sarah right? Is Shirley flirting with him? A few nights later he dreams about Shirley. The memory of that dream makes him glow even during the day. He starts to watch her. Is that smile just for him or does she smile that way at everybody? He closely registers the small, seemingly random touches that make him shudder deliciously.

Sometimes I can hardly stop writing. The story evolves on its own. Occasionally, my fingers on the keyboard can barely follow my thoughts.

Tom returns to the hotel after a day trip. It was hot and he feels dehydrated. Is Sarah already asleep or is she waiting for him with a barrage of accusations? He hates her outbursts. As so often lately, he is reluctant to return to the apartment they share. He orders a drink at the bar and strolls out onto the terrace, taking the glass with him. When he notices two figures in a tight embrace, he walks down the steps to the beach. He does not want to disturb the lovers. No, he cannot stand to watch the happy couple. He sits down on a bench between the palm trees that are closest to the water. A perfect night! Countless stars sparkle on the water in the full moon. The wind rustles softly, merging with the sound of crickets from the nearby bushes. A night for lovers. He is overcome by burning desire, a desire that is sweet yet painful. A crack startles him. Are there steps? A shadow darts in, and the next moment arms wrapp around him. A Giddiness engulfs him, a brief sigh, Shirley ... then soft lips prevent any further word. Their mouths find each other, cling to each other, drink like dying from thirst. Tom staggers after her. He would follow her anywhere, to heaven, to hell, no matter where. The dam is broken. Intoxication has seized him. Everything is so new with Shirley. Tom is overwhelmed.

Did Shirley really fall in love with him? Tom begins to hate the lustful looks of the other men. Jealousy gnaws at him.

»It's mine,« he'd like to call to everyone when Shirley laughs or dances with Ricardo. And she does it often. Again and again, the two are urged on by the audience. The bright red dress nestles softly around Shirley's seductive body. How firmly Ricardo holds her and how deeply he looks into her eyes. Shirley clearly enjoys the excitement she triggers. She is pure sensuality, wrapping her shapely legs around Ricardo, heating up the mood. They act like a couple. Had she also belonged to him? Is she still with him? Can this woman only love one man and can that be me? These questions torment Tom between the intoxicating encounters with Shirley. She laughs at him. »I love you, but a woman is not a piece of land you can own.« She's right-and yet. If it was just a game for her, a flirtation, another conquest, if one day she'd had enough of him, would she then leave him? Then he would die. Only in her arms, does he feels safe. No, Shirley is not easy to explain. She is deep and he threatens to drown in her.

6

I'm surprised by the development. My characters act quite differently than I had planned. They develop a life of their own and turn everything upside down. Have I given them too much freedom? Didn't I pay enough attention? I'm confused. I had intended Shirley to take on the role of a pretty but ruthless bitch. Although she plays this role quite well, I like her. I'm surprised to find that the purposeful way in which she ensnares Tom doesn't bother me. On the contrary, I admire the way Shirley just takes whatever she wants. I even find excuses for her behavior. Sarah, on the other hand, acts like an accomplice. She almost drives Tom into Shirley's arms. Her constant bickering starts to annoy even me. Shirley is beautiful, vivacious and always in a good mood. How could Tom decide differently? Shirley is a woman who seems immune to all hostility. Whom does she remind me of? Do I know any woman like her?

Suddenly I remember that evening in November of last year. Rita had said she was coming. She finally wanted to introduce Robert to Dan and me. I cooked an Italian dinner, as I usually do on occasions like this one, and Dan make jokes about who she was going to present to us as her Mister Right this time and how long it would take her to turn it all into another big drama. The doorbell rang and Rita whirled in, dressed up in a red dress I had never seen before. Her blue eyes sparkled like those of a victorious torero. She just looked stunning.

Now I realize that it was the same red dress Shirley wears when dancing the tango. Then I saw him. Tall, so incredibly tall, and dark-haired with eyes that were almost black. They glowed like burning embers. Immediately I felt mousy. I fled into the kitchen with the excuse to put the flowers in the water. I was totally confused. So that was her photographer, that new man of her dreams she'd talked about endlessly in the last few weeks. I had barely listened; she had raved about men too often before, men who'd disappeared again in no time. But this man had nothing in common with the wanna-be lady killers she had previously introduced to us. The conversation flowed while we ate. They praised my cooking. Rita admired the variety of antipasti I had prepared, and Robert loved the tagliatelle in mushroom cream sauce. I talked about how much I had traveled before I moved in with Dan and raved about Rome, where I had discovered my love for Italian cuisine.

»And instead of Rome, you're just roaming through the international kitchen now?« Robert asked.

»Not just that; I write, too,« I answered hastily.

»Don't you miss travelling?« he inquired.

Surprised, Rita looked up, and I felt Dan's back stiffen.

»Traveling and a relationship can be very difficult to reconcile in the long run,« I said quietly.

The mood had changed.

»They've been through these eternal breakups long enough,« Rita said into the silence. Robert responded with a smile that I couldn't read. My feelings towards Robert fluctuated between rejection and fascination. Rita hadn't noticed. She was happy, purring contentedly.

And now Rita had put her imprint on my Shirley. How could that happen? Did I draw the figure of Shirley too inaccurately? Even Sarah barely resembles the cheerful young woman from the beach I had taken as her role model. And Tom? It shocks me to realize that Tom looks just like Robert.

I leave the house to get away. But I can't escape. Even outdoors, my thoughts turn in circles.

»Don't be so doggedly, Karen.«

Was that Shirley's voice?

»Does everything always have to go according to your ideas?« Is she making fun of me?

»Instead of wanting to change me, maybe you should start with yourself.«

»Ha, funny! Now my characters are telling me what to do!«

Suddenly I feel as if someone were watching me. I'm startled. He's standing right in front of me as if he just grew out of the sand. He's only a few yards away from me and completely nude. A shaggy mop of hair frames his face, which is half concealed by a wild beard. His gray eyes are staring at me. My throat is suddenly dry and my pulse is racing. There is no one else around. What does he want from me? I am terrified yet fascinated. I feel threatened by and at the same time attracted to his wild naturalness. For a moment I am petrified; then I turn around and quickly walk back to the cottage. I feel his eyes on my back for what seems an eternity. I wonder if he's following me but I dare not turn around. I only turn around when I've come close to the other people. He didn't follow me; I can see him as a tiny dot in the distance, and soon he has disappeared. I can't forget that encounter. Was he an exhibitionist who wanted to get off on scaring me? Or was he just a hardened nature lover who didn't mean any harm? If he was, would he have looked at me like that? Over and over again these piercing eyes pop into my mind. I feel as if this lonely nude man had actually exposed a part of me.

Since that day I no longer dare to walk so far. I don't tell anyone about this encounter.

A letter from Rita has arrived in Bath. That surprises me. She has never written to me before. Rita doesn't write letters. She either calls or sends postcards. I only know her handwriting from her short notes in the editorial office. There must be an important reason for her to write a letter. Maybe her love affair with Robert is over. Or their relationship is troubled. Hastily I open the envelope, unfold the pastel-colored stationery and scan the lines in Rita's childlike round, even handwriting. Rita only writes about trivialities, insignificant banal stuff. Why did she write at all? Then she gets a bit more specific: She admonishes me for not visiting her on even one single weekend and not announcing any visits in the near future either.

Robert told me about the indian summer, about the blue sky and the golden yellow and red colors of the maple forests. I can imagine that that's quite enchanting for a weekend – but months in this loneliness?

Robert says ... Robert thinks, Robert ... Robert ... Robert. No, their relationship obviously isn't in trouble. On the contrary, it kind of seems to me that Robert has become even more important to her. I'm losing my patience. »Come on, Rita, why are you really writing?« Talking about things has never been her style. I quickly scan the next lines.

Dan is feeling really down. We're trying to cheer him up but without any success. I think he has completely buried himself in his work. Karen, this man loves you more than anything else. Doesn't that mean anything to you? Believe me, I'd be happy if Robert ever showed me his love like that. Aren't you afraid that you may be risking everything? I admire your courage, but maybe your decision was too final? Come back if you have even the slightest doubt. Everything you can do there, you can do here, too. Remember, the indian summer won't last forever, and what comes next is a long, cold, lonely winter. Anyway, you're being missed in Boston. We'd like to have you back here with us. Didn't you promise to come see us periodically? If you can't make up your mind, we'll come to you.

So that's it. Dan is behind it. I'm angry and somehow disappointed. It annoys me that Rita is trying to interfere. Besides, she's my friend. She probably didn't notice all the times Dan made fun of her. But I sense that there's something else, too. My disappointment can't be explained just by this letter. Rita no longer acts like a true friend to me. I keep annoying her. We've become strangers. After going to Globus, I changed. Rita, it seems to me, has become increasingly childish and naïve. Sometimes I can hardly endure her prattle, her stories about insignificant little scandals in the editorial office, her recurring complaints that she would like to get married but that Robert isn't ready for marriage, doesn't even want to live with her. Today it's her constant Robert says and Robert thinks that upsets me.

I decide not to call Dan.

»Problems?« Grace interrupts my thoughts.

»I don't know. I have no idea, Grace. Maybe.«

7

On my way home I feel miserable. No, I don't want them to come see me, I couldn't take it. I can't imagine Rita or Robert in my current life. Dan might even come along. Or at least they'd describe his grief to me in a very colorful way. They'd talk to me and try to convince me to come back. They'd look at this little cottage, compare it to my spacious home in Boston. They'd mess up my daily routine, my whole rhythm.

A few days later I decide to go to Boston. I take the same way I took two months ago. On the trip my whole body starts to tingle. I'm scared of what to expect. What will Dan look like? On the phone his voice always sounded so tired and sad. Will I have to listen to accusations? Will they harass me until I have to struggle for air?

On the outskirts of Boston the traffic is increasing significantly. I'm no longer used to this hustle and bustle. At least the sun shines peacefully. It is a gentle autumn sun, all in delicate pastel colors. Maybe it won't be as bad as I think.

Leo complains quietly. He was extremely reluctant to go into his basket. Despite the sedative drops I gave him before the trip he became restless several times. Maybe he didn't get enough drops because he was struggling so much. Perhaps the remedy no longer works as well because he is so much stronger now?

»We're almost there; then you can get out of your cage.«

I won't say the word »home.« It is just after two p.m. Dan will be impatient. Actually, I wanted to be there at one but I left later than I had planned. There was still work to do. Trying on different outfits occupied me for quite a long time because my everyday clothes, which I have worn almost constantly for the past few weeks, seemed inappropriate for Boston. On the other hand, I didn't feel comfortable in the costume either. So I stayed with the jeans. Then I had to water the kitchen herbs, rinse a cup and two glasses. I also wanted to stop by at Grace's. But basically everything was just to postpone the trip. I can picture Dan now going back and forth impatiently between the living room and the kitchen. The thought makes me even more nervous. He knows me as reliable and punctual. I almost run the last few feet to the front door so as if I could make up for lost time. Before I push the bell, I take a deep breath. Dan opens the door. His face is flushed. He's excited, and obviously he's been very worried.

»I'm sorry, but ...«

»Come in!« he says, wiping away any other words with his hand as he takes me into his arms. They cling to me tightly and don't let me go for an eternity. He kisses me hungrily. I feel like I'm trapped in a vice. At the moment, the feeling of distress revitalizes me. Where is the sensual, soft, warm desire of the past? Even today, Dan's body is warm, no, almost hot. He is sweating. I'm uncomfortable. Nothing is true, everything is different from what it used to be. His embrace does not make me feel strong but despairing.

I struggle out of his embrace.

»You have become so fragile,« he says. »You probably don't eat enough.«

Can't he see that I look radiant? I study his face. The man I thought I knew so well suddenly looks so different. I can't tell what has changed. His features look more edgy. Has he lost weight? Suddenly I have a vision of what he will look like when he is old. Now that the frantic flush has subsided, his skin looks pale.

»I have to free Leo from his cage.« I turn away from him. I know I'm not allowed to talk about Maine now. It seems almost impossible to rave about my beach walks. How it would hurt him to hear that I was better off without him and making good progress in writing.

Leo shoots out of the basket like a bullet, looks around in amazement and disappears under the sofa.

»What was that? Leo! Don't you know where you are ?«

»He'll come out when he's hungry.« Dan shrugs. »What do you want, darling?« he suddenly says in an inappropriately cheerful tone. »Coffee, cake, a glass of champagne?«

»Maybe one of each,« I reply with relief, glad of any distraction. »I'll make coffee.«

»No,« he says, holding me back, »of course *I* will.« He leads me emphatically to the armchair.

»Should I sit down and be served?«

»Why not? Just sit down or freshen up or unpack your bag.«

»Okay.« I give in and disappear in the bathroom. What a contrast it is to the bathroom in the beach cottage! This space, almost three times the size of my bathroom in the cottage, looks almost bombastic with its green ivy border on the white tiles, the brass fittings and the large crystal mirror. It exudes such cool elegance. I don't fit into this setting and decide to change clothes and apply make-up after all.

In the walk-in closet between the bathroom and the bedroom, I can choose my outfit from a 10-feet wide closet crammed with clothes. When did I ever wear all this stuff? In Maine, I've got only five pairs of jeans and a few sweaters and blouses. Plus I took a chic suit and a skirt with me that I 've never worn yet. In here, it's like the warehouse of a department store. I check out many different clothes without being able to make a decision. I pull something out here and there but then I put it back.

»Karen, what's taking you so long?«

»Just a minute!« I quickly opt for off-white gabardine pants and an ice blue sweater, colors I particularly like. Nevertheless, I feel strange and somehow disguised in my clothes. It's like I'm disappearing into them. Everything's a bit too big for me. The energy and vitality of the last few weeks also seemed to have fallen away from me as soon as I took off my everyday clothes.

Dan has set the dining table. A huge bouquet of dark red roses is sitting next to the simple white dishes. He comes up to me with a glass of champagne.

»Oh, Dan ...«

»Welcome back, darling.« Dan hands me the glass and fixes me with his gaze. He has obviously calmed down, feels safer again. His nervous fussiness is gone. Now he leads me to the table. A flat square cardboard box, artfully wrapped, is sitting on my plate.

»What's that? It's not my birthday – is there something else to celebrate?«

»Do you always need a reason for a gift?«

He watches me expectantly while I open the box. My hunch is confirmed. The wrapping paper reveals an elaborately designed plastic box with the filigree gold letters of the exclusive jewelry shop Pollack & Sons. When I open it, my heart stops. A white-gold necklace with a brilliant aquamarine heart sparkles in my hand. Dan puts the necklace around my neck. I feel uncomfortable. It's beautiful, but such an expensive gift feels like an obligation, a bribe.

Suddenly the conversation has reached an impasse; we no longer know what to talk about. What *did* we talk about? My job, his job, my parents, food, going out somewhere? Dan wants to ignore the last two months; for me they are more real than this house and our relationship.

»This time, it seems to work for Rita,« he suddenly starts on a subject that seems innocuous to him.

»What?« I don't really know what he's talking about.

»Rita and Robert – they're still together. Who would've thought it possible that it could work out this time? I mean, Robert and her being so different.«

»You're right.« In my mind, I picture the two of them: Robert tall and always a bit mysterious, Rita petite, her heart on her sleeve.

»Rita's very much looking forward to seeing you. She was the one who planned the dinner with me and contributed something to it.«

I'm amazed. »What were you planning? That sounds exciting.«

»Italian, but I won't reveal any more than that. Definitely something out of the ordinary.«

As if on cue, the phone suddenly rings. The glaring sound that is no longer unfamiliar to me, startles me. It's Rita. She wants to know if I'm there.

»Yes, she arrived an hour and a half ago. No, I didn't reveal anything ... I think so... Yes, she's doing fine ...« Dan's gaze rests on me, smiling. What's that all about? In the past, Rita and Dan accepted each other but weren't exactly friends. By now they seem to understand each other really well.

»Of course, just ask her. She's sitting next to me.«

»Hello, Rita.«

»Karen, nice that you're there. How do you feel, back in civilization? Dan, and of course we, too, were so happy to hear that you were coming. How do you like your gift?« Rita asks breathlessly and without any pause. She obviously doesn't expect an answer.

»Okay, see you around eight then.«

»My goodness, Rita's even more hectic than she used to be.«

»You think so? Oh, this is only because you haven't talked to her for quite a while,« Dan says. Leo ventures cautiously towards the food bowl. He blinks at us, unsettled. We watch his unusual behavior in silence. Without loosening up, he devours his food, starting at every sound.

»He's acting strange.«

»He's just not used to this environment. Maybe he doesn't re-member it,« I try to defend my furry friend. Dan approaches him, wanting to caress him, but Leo escapes to his safe hiding place. I think of my small, sun-drenched beach cottage, the door that stays open in the day time so that Leo can easily push it open and disappear into his hunting grounds as he pleases. The massive walls here in Boston feel like a fortress, a bunker that blocks light, air and sun. No, Leo will never get used to this house again, and I suspect it won't be any different for me.

I get up from the table and go to the seating group.

»Leo, come here,« I try to lure the scared animal.

»Just leave him alone.« Dan followed me. He wraps his arms around me from behind and tries to pull me onto the chair. »Forget about the cat for now,« he whispers hoarsely in my ear. He presses his hot lips on my cheek and my mouth. The unexpected attack triggers fear and severe heart palpitations. Dan feels like a stranger to me.

»Dan, please, I'm suffocating.«

»I love you, Karen, I love you.«

Tears shoot into my eyes. What did I expect? Did I really think he would be happy to just sit across from me, drinking coffee and talking to me? And what about the night? I'd love to escape. Like Leo, I want to crawl into a corner. For a moment, I'm considering just letting it go to avoid an unpleasant discussion. My legs feel numb. I get up and pull myself away from him. If I give in now, I'll give up everything. Then I won't ever be able again to fight anything. Dan has moved back from me, breathing hard.

»Dan, I haven't really arrived yet. Give me some time.«

»Sure, I'll give you all the time in the world.« He gets up, walks over to the dinner table and empties a full glass of champagne with a few gulps. Then he looks at me. »You want some, too?«

»Yes, sure.« I don't want to give him another rejection. He pours another glass for himself, too, clinking glasses while he gazes deeply and searchingly into my eyes.

»To our future, Karen!« I just nod.

Dan disappears in the kitchen to prepare the meal. No, he doesn't want me to join him in the kitchen. »Just get comfortable,«

he suggests when my helpless gaze follows him to the kitchen. Again I try to lure Leo out of his hiding place. How I would've loved to hold him close to me and bury my face in his fur. But he won't budge. I decide to rinse away my discomfort in the shower. After that, it'll be best for me to change clothes again.

I'm in the shower for a small eternity. The hot water feels soothing, and the noise of the gushing water shields me from everything. I focus intensively on my body, taking a lot of time. I rub my face until it tingles. I rub body lotion all over my body, brush my teeth long and thoroughly, blow my hair dry. Again, I find myself standing in front of the wardrobe, staring at my clothes. It takes me a long time to select a short, slender gray dress. I even put on makeup – for the first time in months – and apply one of the many perfumes I've collected. Now I feel better. Gazing into the mirror, I look a bit like a stranger, but I do feel prepared for the evening.

Dan is thrilled. I can see it in his eyes. He quickly picks up the white-gold necklace and puts it around my neck. It looks beautiful, and yet I would rather not wear it. I feel literally chained up. The doorbell rings, our guests have arrived. Rita, exuberantly cheerful, noisily fills the whole room. What a relief after Dan's and my stalled conversation! Now it feels a bit like it used to be.

Robert smiles at me. Rita pats Dan's arm unusually buddy-buddy-like and disappears with him into kitchen, carrying two bowls. I'm staying alone in the living room with Robert. Damn, this man is handsome.

»Karen, you look dazzling. Did you actually work in Maine? You look like you've just come back from your vacation.«

»I am working, and I feel great.«

»Yes, Maine is glorious, especially at this time of year. I've already made recordings there. Maybe I should go there again; then I could visit you. You want me to visit you?«

»You wouldn't find it. The cottage is completely secluded.«

»I would find it. You wanna bet? I always find everything. Or don't you believe me?« His eyes burn into mine. I blush. Is he flirting with me? Does he like to confuse me? Or is it real, does he really mean *me*? Ah, no! He's probably one of these men who flirt with every woman.

»Sit down. You want an aperitif?« I ask to conceal my insecurity.

»Let's wait for the others.«

I sit down with him.

»Have you been on the road a lot lately?« I try to start a neutral conversation.

He ignores my question. »Will you come back, Karen? I mean, come back here, to Dan?«

I wasn't prepared for that question. »At the moment, I'm mainly busy with my book.«

»But in spring, Karen – what are you going to do then?«

Fortunately Rita and Dan come out of the kitchen with a tray full of carefully decorated appetizers, so I don't have to answer that question.

Dan opens a bottle of white wine and fills our glasses. We cheer and have some small-talk. It's harmless. Inconsequential. I can hardly concentrate on what the others are saying. The things Robert just said go through my head. Could it be, could it be? I throw him a furtive glance. Our eyes meet, lock, and all of a time I know that it has happened.

Rita just said something. What was it? Help, where am I? I hastily grab my glass. Robert saves me.

»To you, Karen. To your book and your success.«

»Oh yeah, what about your book – are you getting on with it?« Rita inquires. She doesn't seem to sense how uncomfortable that subject makes Dan.

»Yes, it's going pretty well,« I say, noticing that Rita isn't really like Shirley in my book. That reassures me.

Dan doesn't like the new direction our conversation has taken at all. I can distinctly feel it.

»Speaking of food, I'll check on it,« he says, distracting from the subject.

»You want me to help you?« Rita offers immediately.

»Not yet, maybe later.«

The ease of the conversation has evaporated.

»Dan still doesn't accept it,« I say.

»But Karen, of course he doesn't! Of course he wants you to be with him. I think he's terribly lonely. Aren't you fed up with living in the wilderness?« Rita seems unusually engaged.

»Rita, you know that I promised Clifford to inhabit the house all winter.«

»I know, but that doesn't mean you really have to stay that long. We also expected you to come to Boston on a regular basis. Now you're even less at home than when you were traveling for Globus. I can really understand that it irritates Dan.«

»Well, Rita, Karen knows what she's doing,« Robert says.

»Only you can talk like that. You don't know what it means for those who are staying behind, waiting. Dan's suffering, and I can understand him.«

»There are people who are not made for a regular life. I think this stay in Maine is important for Karen.«

»You can't just think of yourself when you're in a relationship. It puts the relationship at risk. Dan must think she no longer loves him.«

»So what, Rita? It's none of our business.«

»Robert, how can you talk like that? You know how unbearable this situation is for Dan.«

»Well, you could comfort him,« Robert interrupts her zeal. Rita wants to reciprocate, but instead she gets up and rushes away into the kitchen.

»Sorry for that, Karen. In moments like this one I can understand only too well that you've run away,« Robert says.

»I didn't run away; I just left to work in peace.«

»Come on – you don't need to fool me.«

»Don't you start on me now, too. Just leave me alone. I don't wanna talk about it.« Tears form in my eyes. Robert suddenly gets up and comes to me. Sitting next to me, he puts his arm around my shoulder and gently turns my face to him with his other hand.

»I understand you, don't you know? I understand you all too well.« His gaze is unusually serious. His words melt something inside of me. Any resistance I had dissolves. Robert wipes a tear from the corner of my eye just as it begins to fall. Surprised, I allow the delicate touch to happen. And while he caresses my cheek, his eyes are coming closer, his lips are sealing my mouth. Then his kiss erases all perception. I just know I want it, and I've been wanting it forever.

Rita's energetic steps, echoing from the kitchen, call me back to the present. Robert briefly holds me close; then he calmly returns to his seat . I get up hastily and disappear into the bathroom. I stare into the mirror. My face is glowing and my heart is beating hard. It's real, it's real, it's real, my heart is hammering. I'm totally confused. In order not to destroy my make-up, I hold both forearms in the cold water and cool myself off. I still feel Robert's kiss on my lips.

»Karen, dinner's ready,« I hear Dan's voice calling me.

»Just a minute.« I hastily powder my nose and cheeks and apply more lipstick.

As if she were the hostess, Rita has set the table together with Dan. I'm astonished by this new alliance. When I think of how Dan used to talk about Rita… A crazy thought flashes through my mind: Why aren't they a couple? They both want to get married, and then Robert and I would be free. The idea startles me. Is this what I want? And how can I get Robert to want that? What does he want? I look at him briefly. He sits across from me at the dinner table. Our eyes meet again. I quickly look at Rita and Dan; they don't seem to notice anything. They're too busy presenting their three-course meal.

After a tasty combination of green lettuces with shrimp and a herb dressing, they serve tender veal schnitzel with leafy spinach, parmesan and tagliatelle with a light white wine. The food tastes delicious, but my appetite isn't great. The room is filled with a bittersweet, crackling tension and at the same time a dark, velvety pain. Something new, overwhelming, not yet tangible is in the air. And I feel that something that has been an important part of my life for a long time is over, irretrievably over. Wistfulness and sorrow overshadow my mood. Never before have I experienced a sense of farewell pain and expectant tingling so close to each other. I drink a little too much and too fast, and at some point Rita and I behave like the giggling young journalists of the Salem Post. I enjoy this state of tipsy lightness, and Dan also seems to feel positive about this turnaround. He smiles paternally forgivingly while Robert is watching us thoughtfully.

At some point, Robert urges to leave. All of a sudden I feel exhausted. And I'm afraid to be alone with Dan. Not without reason. As soon as the front door has closed behind the two of them, he comes to me, and I know exactly what he wants, despite the alcohol that fogs my mind. I nervously step back a few feet and look at him uneasily. He registers it and puts his arm around my shoulder.

»Another glass of wine, sweetheart?«

I nod, glad for any delay. If we drink more wine, he may also get tired and fall asleep soon. So we empty a few more glasses. I praise his food. He compliments me on my looks.

»You're getting along fantastically with Rita lately,« I say.

»Who cares about Rita now?« he says.

»I always though you didn't really like her. But today it looked as if you were close friends.«

»Kiss me.« His face is close to me, his mouth is whispering into my ear, then he caresses me with his tongue. His hot breath approaches my face. I give him my mouth, wanting to soothe him with my kisses. I'll talk to him later. He greedily presses his mouth on my lips. He can no longer patronize me, I still think. His tongue is deep in my mouth, his hands are holding my head tight, so I can't dodge. I hope... His whole body is hovering over me, holding me tight with his arms and legs, uttering words and sighs between the kisses, sounds I don't understand. Pillows rustle next to my ear. Somewhere, fabric is ripping. His fingers are everywhere, he tugs at me, his hands are between my thighs. My body resists him. Suddenly I see someone else's black eyes. I feel someone else's lips on my mouth. They burn ...

»No!« I scream. With all the strength I have, I push him away.

»I don't want it, I don't want it, can't you tell?« I scream at him like I have never before.

Dan stares at me aghast. A vein in his neck starts to vibrate visible. His face is reddening. I am totally quiet, watching the strange face in front of me.

»What's wrong with you, Karen? What is it? Is there someone else? Come on, tell me the truth! Is there somebody in your beach house? Or maybe there is no beach house at all but just another guy? Is he better than me?« His voice almost gags. »Can he offer you more than me?«

»No! You're doing too much for me. You make me sick, and now you make me sick, and now even this necklace, too.« I undo the lock with trembling fingers and throw it at him.

Dan freezes; he downs another glass of wine, carefully picks up the chain, places it on the table and walks to the door.

»Listen to me! We have to talk!« I call after him.

»Not today, Karen, not today, I don't want to fight, not in those few hours we have together.«

»You never want to talk about anything!« But he's already disappeared into bathroom. I sit in the silent room, feeling sober and awake despite the alcohol. Without thinking, I start to take dishes and glasses into the kitchen. A few minutes later Dan stands in the doorway.

»Just leave it; I'll do it tomorrow.«

»I can't sleep now.«

He leaves again. I move slowly, take a lot of time, carry each piece individually into the kitchen and put it in the dishwasher. I hope Dan will just go to bed and fall asleep right away. When I don't hear another sound, I go to the bathroom.

When I lie down in the bed next to him without turning on the light, Dan's even breath and quiet snoring tell me that he really is asleep. I long to fall asleep soon, too. But I keep staying awake. Again and again I see a face, a face with dark brown eyes. "I love you," a tender voice whispers into my ear. No, that's not true, he didn't say that. I understand you, I understand you only too well, he said, and then he kissed me. But doesn't that mean the same thing? Again and again I feel his kiss. I picture his long, slim hands touching me. I long for him, for his tenderness. It's been so long since I have enjoyed a passionate hug. Strictly speaking, I can't even remember the last one.

Suddenly I'm terrified. Rita is my friend. What have I done? Even if our friendship is no longer as intense as it used to be, a love affair between Robert and me is absolutely out of the question. I myself had advised Rita against him when she complained about his many travels, his frequent absence.

»He's not a man for a solid relationship. He will never belong to only you. He's not a man you can start a family with.« How old-fashioned, how abhorrently reasonable I had talked to her! And now I want this man for myself.

8

I can't stand another minute in bed, and so I get up and sneak out of the room. Leo comes to greet me. I pour some cream into his bowl and sit down on the couch in the living room. What new, additional chaos am I getting myself into right now? I left Dan and talked about freedom and independence, about self-realization by writing my book. Now I'm about to fall in love with a man my rational mind tells me to stay away from. Or have I loved him for a long time? The situation horrifies and agitates me. I scour the bathroom cupboard for a sleeping pill and rinse it down with a big gulp of water. I want to forget, I don't want to have to think any more. I turn on the TV. Pictures flicker on the TV screen. I can hardly focus on them but they distract me. Leo cuddles up to me. I wait until the sleeping pill makes my limbs feel heavy. Then I go back to bed.

What time is it? Slowly, sounds start to penetrate through the wall the pill has erected. The alcohol I drank tonight gives me a slight headache. Waking up is unpleasant. The noise of engines and honking horns penetrates my ear drums. I miss the familiar sound of the waves and the cries of the seagulls. Only slowly do I start to understand where I am. The bed next to me is empty. The scent of coffee. Nevertheless, I turn over again.

What was that strange dream about? I try to remember the images: I was in a huge palace, walking up a wide staircase. Actually, it wasn't a real building at all. The walls and the roof consisted of filigree metal rods. In fact it resembled a huge cage. I moved through the airy hall in amazement. Birds were fluttering around, and suddenly there were white, dancing snowflakes everywhere. They weren't cold, and I was amazed to discover that they were white petals swirling through the air. The bars were rusted in many places, some of them were broken, grasses and flowers grew everywhere. I left the house that was about to disintegrate.

It was a wonderful dream. The house, the sun, the transparent structure, the birds sailing freely through the air, and the snow that turned into petals. But I was alone, and that depressed me. Robert! How obvious it would have been to meet him in a dream. How much I would've liked some indication, a positive view of the future! Instead, there was only this emptiness and loneliness.

The house I fell asleep in has not disintegrated. It encloses me firmly and relentlessly. I want to slip under the duvet and wake up in Maine. I know this is not going to happen, so I decide not to delay getting up and meeting Dan any longer. It's already eleven. Perhaps we can have a talk today.

Dan is in the kitchen. He had already cleaned up and made breakfast. He turns to me kindly, as if nothing had happened. He looks miserable. Instead of self-pity, I have hot pangs of guilt. Leo is totally confused. Dan wants to let him out. Horrified, I respond, »No, as panicky as he is, he'd run into the next car.« Amazingly, Leo lets me pick him up. Watching me, Dan says, »I'm sorry I overwhelmed you last night, darling. It was a mistake, I know.« While his arms dangle helplessly, his eyes are one single pleading hug.

»Accept my gift. Don't take away my hope that everything will be good again.« His contriteness robs me of any courage to talk openly to him. What can I say to him anyway? Dan, I don't love you anymore, I fell in love with my girlfriend's boyfriend? Even though Robert is not capable of a relationship and probably not faithful, either, I still long for his tenderness, while I can no longer bear yours. I can't live with you any more; I cannot marry you and become a housewife and the mother of your children. Right now I don't know *what* I want.

I don't say any of this but accept the cup of coffee he gives me, take it to the bathroom, swallow an aspirin to make my headache go away and take a shower. While the water is drumming down on me, I think of my trip back home. This time tomorrow I'll already be on the road again. Strange, after just two months I call that place my home. I can suddenly smell the sun-warmed wood of the house and the sea. This is where I want to be. I miss Grace. I can see her austere face and hear her calm, sober voice. Yes, Grace will help me sort out my feelings. Thinking of her soothes me.

After I've dressed, I put on some make-up. Then we go to the city to grab a bite to eat. The air is fresh, and the warm golden autumn sun has lured many people outside. Everyone seems to be in good spirits. We stroll through the Public Garden and the Common towards the city center. The store windows are decorated with ghosts, skeletons, witch masks and pumpkin faces for Halloween. At Quincy Market, we run into people wearing masks. They were probably coming from one of the numerous parades. The mostly creepy, sometimes deadly-serious faces greatly contrast the cheerful dances. A clown sways towards me, grinning as if he wanted to mock me. He links arms with me and pulls me along several feet. The hustle and bustle is getting denser and denser; we escape into the Margarita. Did Dan pick it intentionally? It all started right here. Is this the grand finale? Is he hoping that there'll be a new beginning for us? We try to talk about trivial things. Our gestures and looks are clumsy, and most of them freeze somewhere in the air. It's exhausting, but it seems even more dangerous to be silent.

In the evening Dan is strangely quiet. When I talk to him, he responds warmly, but he doesn't try very hard to keep up a conversation. He looks at the TV screen with apparent interest. Soon I, too, fall silent. The feeling of wistfulness and sorrow that already feels all too familiar spreads in my body. It hurts.

A shrill ringing sound pierces the dull silence. Rita's on the phone; she wants to say goodbye to me. This time even she seems to sense the dark mood through the phone line.

»Is everything okay with you guys?« she asks.

»Yeah, yeah, I'm just tired,« I say, fending her off. »Sure, I'll call you.«

She doesn't mention Robert with one single word. After hanging up, I walk into the bathroom, swallow two sleeping pills and wipe my make-up off. Before I go to bed, I briefly put my hand on Dan's shoulder and wish him a good night. He turns to me, looks at me thoughtfully, says »good night« without touching me. In bed, I pull the blanket over my head and cry myself to sleep.

Our farewell in the morning is short. Dan lets me go after a fleeting hug without uttering any reproaches. I am grateful to him for that. Relieved, I leave the raging city and am glad when I've reached the highway.

9

»Leo, we're going home.« My mortally offended cat doesn't respond.

When I arrive at the weathered cottage, I feel as if I had been away for several weeks. Even Leo purrs enthusiastically. Will he ever settle down again anywhere else? Delighted by the freedom he has regained, he disappears into the pine scrub behind the house. For Leo, the world is okay again.

It's not that easy for me. The weekend in Boston has left me confused. The illusion that a temporary separation from Dan would improve our relationship has dissipated. The rupture between him and me is deeper than I ever thought possible. The separation is final. Suddenly I realize that this is precisely the decision I made in the last few days. The sudden realization of finality almost takes my breath away. Is Dan as clearly aware of it as I am? How am I supposed to let him know? Panic grips me. The future is a black hole that threatens to engulf me.

The next day I go to Bath. I long for Grace. Compared to the loneliness around my beach house, there is a lot going on in Bath, but compared to Boston it is relaxed and manageable. After my routine shopping, I enter the Intown pub, and it feels like coming home from a long journey. The wood-panelled, cozy restaurant now seems to be the only constant in my life. How nice it is to see Grace behind the counter again.

»Karen!« She is happy to see me and hugs me warmly. Then she pulls a bit away from me and looks me over.

»What was it like in Boston? You don't look all that happy. How did it go?«

I can feel tears in my eyes. »Oh Grace, it was horrible. I feel bad, worse than before,« and my tears already start to flow.

»Come on, sit down. I'll get some coffee. Or do you need something stronger?«

»No, coffee's fine.« I smile, tormented.

She fills two large cups and sits down across from me.

»Now tell me: What was so horrible?«

»Well, horrible isn't really the word for it. No, the weekend wasn't horrible. What's horrible is that I couldn't clarify anything.«

»Couldn't you talk to each other?«

»Oh Grace, Dan is either absolutely clueless – or he doesn't *want* to see what's going on. Yes, that's probably it. He just doesn't want to *know*. He didn't ask me what's on my mind, not what's bothering me, not how I live here, what my daily routine is, how my book is coming along. Nothing, nothing, nothing! All he noticed was that I lost some weight.«

»Did he at least like that?«

»It didn't sound like it. He rather sounded as if I was bad off if he didn't take care of me.«

»Ah yes, so he thinks you can't take care of yourself. Well, then he doesn't know you at all, does he?«

»That's just Dan's way of showing me his love. And everyone really tried their best. It was amazing,« I blurt out, sobbing. When I can talk again, I tell her the whole story, from the stilted welcome, the roses, the expensive necklace to the meal planned and cooked by Dan and Rita with love and Dan's caring ways in general.

»Grace, you're right, he treats me like a child. And this time I felt it was particularly bad. Every minute of the day was planned. I was a puppet, with everyone pulling on my strings. Yet I didn't manage to complain about it. It was also very touching and certainly well-intentioned. And I feel it's partly my fault that Dan's so unhappy.«

In the end, Grace knows everything – apart from that incident with Robert. There's something that makes me hide that secret. I don't think Grace would understand it. Sound, practical, unsentimental Grace. I'm afraid she might condemn me for that. On the other hand, I can well imagine her vigorously sweeping it away, saying, »Girl, don't look for the next problem.« And, »Men always mean trouble.« She said that to me when we first met.

Though I suspect she's right, I'm not prepared to give up my secret dream. In my mind, I can see his black eyes all too clearly. Many things he said last year now take on a very different meaning. And again and again I can feel his kiss. Even if this sweet secret is the only thing that has remained, it is more than anything that has happened to me for a long time.

Grace strokes my hand, which nervously plays with a napkin. »I'll be back in a second.« She gets up to fetch the coffee pot; then she fills our cups again.

»Grace, why is life, why are relationships, so difficult?«

»Don't feel down, girl. It won't always be that way. Perhaps more has been clarified than you think now.«

Questioning, I look at Grace. Does she know I'm hiding something from her? But I don't read anything like that in her face. It's as kind as always. That reassures me. Losing her as a friend would be a disaster. My life is difficult enough as it is.

The weekend in Boston has set me back. Everything has changed. I can't resume my usual daily routine. I've also stopped my daily swimming exercises. Although I was quite used to it before I left, the water is now too cold for me. I can't continue working on my book. It almost seems to me as if Sarah, Tom and Shirley had also gone on a trip and haven't returned yet.

I clean up in the house, cook my meals, drink coffee or try to read. When I can no longer sit because of my inner tension and start pacing in my room like a trapped wild animal, it's time to go out into the fresh air. The sea has always been the best way to soothe my restlessness. The powerful waves rolling to the shore give me a sense of permanence, while everything else seems to change constantly.

10

The days are getting shorter. When I wake up, it's still dark outside, and the twilight starts early again. The colors have faded as if a delicate veil had settled over everything. There are less and less people on the beach. Only a few days later, thick clouds cover the sky that is usually blue. A strong wind whirls along the shore. The waves pile up as high as mountains and crash against the shore. The indian summer is finally over.

I know from Grace that we can expect snow starting in mid-November. Suddenly I realize that I need to buy supplies as soon as possible. Grace had told me about winters in which you were snowed in for days and all the streets became impassable.

My shopping list is long. In addition to the usual food supplies, I get a large supply of canned goods. I also buy lots of cat food, several cans of coffee and boxes of tea, matches and candles. I get paper for the printer at the stationery store and books at the bookstore: three novels – two new publications and an 800-page classic I've been wanting to read for ages. The car is packed. Physically, at least, I'm well prepared for a longer blizzard.

When I step into the pub after my shopping tour, Grace looks at me expectantly.

»And – did you have a visitor?«

»No, why?«

»Well, someone called here a few days ago and asked for you.«

»Who?« I ask, surprised, immediately thinking of Robert.

»I don't know. Harry was the one who answered the phone. – Harry! Do you know who was asking for Karen the other day?« Grace shouts.

The friendly but not very communicative cook comes out of the kitchen and dries his hands on his apron.

»Harry, what did the caller want who asked for Karen?«

»It was a man. He asked how to get to the house where the young journalist lives. That's all I know.«

»Did he tell you his name, and did you tell him how to get to the cottage?« I interject excitedly.

»I can't remember if he gave me his name. I tried to explain to him how to get there. But I also told him that it's very difficult to find. I told him it would be better to come here. Shouldn't I have said that?« he asks uneasily.

»No, no, it's okay,« I reassure him. Robert, it can only have been Robert, I think.

»Do you have any idea who that could've been?« Grace inquires. »Do you expect anybody?«

»No, I have no idea.« I keep quiet about Robert even though I'm absolutely sure.

Now it's hard for me to keep listening to Grace. What are Robert's intentions? Why didn't he leave a message? Will he call again or just show up on my doorstep one day, the way he announced it, making it sound like a joke?

11

On the way home it feels as if I'm floating. I feel as light as a feather. A sense of hope rises in my chest. Nothing is fixed forever, no path taken is irreversible. New things are possible every day. My heart sings with expectation, unreasonable yet enticingly sweet. A tingle like on Christmas, just before you get your gifts – or before a long-awaited first date.

I push the thought of bad weather and long winter months away, convinced that something wonderful will happen soon. Robert, I can see him, I can feel his hug and taste his kiss. A soft wave engulfs me. Robert, Robert, how can I ever think straight again? I can see him coming towards me. At last. Why did it take us so long? Yes, why couldn't it, why shouldn't it just be like this? With Robert? Why not with him? Throw all the concerns overboard and just jump in. My heart takes a small leap. Just get out of the confusion and into the arms of the man you've been longing for. There it is again, this long-forgotten desire.

I turn off the car and run down to the water without taking the groceries inside. And I play the game I loved so much as a kid. I pretend that what I want is real. I envision it in bright, dazzling colors. Robert is walking next to me along the beach, holding my hand. At times I can feel its tender pressure. »It's beautiful here; I can understand why you're here,« he tells me. I see and feel the sun. We enjoy the breeze that gently blows around us, the seagulls, small silver arrows that fly past us and occasionally utter shrill screams. Our steps are accompanied by the gentle murmur of water.

I tell Robert about the countless hours I have walked on this beach. I tell him about the wind and the storm. About the hot summer days that washed up cheerful people on the shore. How I first met Sarah and Tom here. When we have reached the rocks, we sit down. He puts his arm around me, and we gaze at the distant horizon. We think of Europe, of the world on the other side of the Atlantic. We think about where we would like to be right now. On the Eiffel Tower, with Paris at our feet, on the Croisette in Cannes, or in Rome, perhaps at the Fontana di Trevi where I would throw three coins into the water. That should bring us good luck.

Robert. I can picture him everywhere, tanned, tall and well built. Click, click, click, his camera greedily devours the rich scenes. But the gaze of his brown eyes belongs only to me. I, too, am tanned and radiate happiness. As I used to.

I don't feel the wind, nor do I notice the grey clouds in the sky. Back in the cottage, my euphoric mood continues. The future is a wonderful promise.

After I have put my purchases away, I make myself a cup of tea. Soon we might drink tea together, plan together, pack suitcases together at some point. Going where we like to go, writing and taking pictures. I need to talk to Grace about it. Will she like Robert?

That night I toss and turn forever until I finally fall asleep in the early hours of the morning. It is a restless sleep.

I'm amazed to see Rita. She stands in the dark room like a shadow.

»Rita!«

She looks pale.

»Rita, what're you doing here?« I ask, surprised.

»I want Robert back,« she says in a toneless voice.

»But Robert's not here.«

»Yes, he is. Do you think I didn't know what you two were planning to do? You think I haven't noticed that you were interested in him from the beginning?«

»But, Rita – I left!«

»Yes, because you wanted space. I know what kind of space you were talking about. And I thought you were my friend.« She looks at me contemptuously.

I feel bad and feel a pang of guilt. »I don't know what you're talking about, Rita. Nothing happened, you were always there, anyway.«

»But now you guys want to be alone and you don't want anyone to disturb you.«

»Robert's not here!«

»Do you really think I'm blind and can't see him?«

Now I notice Robert, too; he's sitting on a bench in a dark corner of my bedroom. He watches us like a spectator. Irritated, my gaze wanders back and forth from him to Rita.

»He keeps doing it, he keeps going to see other women, and I have to came and fetch him. Do you have any idea how many times I've already had to do that?«

»You mean when he leaves, he's actually always with other women and not taking any pictures at all?«

»Yes, what did you think?«

I am horrified. »He said that he loves me.«

»And you really believe that?«

»Robert!« I look at him with pleading eyes. »Say something!«

But Robert just shrugs without saying anything.

»By the way, Robert's married,« Rita says coldly.

»And what about you,« I angrily hiss, glaring at Rita, »why are you with him?«

»I'm prepared to share him, but you're not; you want him for yourself.«

I wake up from the nightmare and am drenched in sweat. For several minutes I lie in bed without moving. My body feels leaden. The euphoria of the previous evening has faded. Robert married? Sure, it was just a dream, but what do I know about him? Couldn't it be true? I remember the first time we met. Didn't my mental alarm go off? Maybe this dream just reminded me of what I had known long ago but had preferred to ignore? I think it's quite possible that Robert is married. Yes, I'm pretty sure about it. Or why shouldn't he at least have more girlfriends on the side? After all, he flirted madly with me from the first moment he laid eyes on me. His way of life allows him a double or even multiple lives without too much trouble. My romantic vision has collapsed like a house of cards. Today I'm embarrassed about the childish daydream I indulged in yesterday. How could I just let myself drift like that? I did exactly what I always accused Rita of. I threw all reason overboard. Even if Robert is *not* married and there are no other women in his life, he often stressed that a relationship was no reason for him to change his life. And he has clearly shown in his relationship with Rita that he really means that. Why should he change just because of me? I'm nuts. Perhaps he felt sympathy for the woman who seemed to him to be like him in her desire for freedom and independence, and just offered to be her friend. He was probably just thinking of a nice, uncomplicated friendship while I fell back into my earliest teenage dreams.

How simple and uncomplicated it had been with Dan from the start. I didn't have to puzzle over the seriousness of our relationship. Why has all this no longer been enough for me? Perhaps there is no such thing as great, lasting happiness at all, or I'm just not capable of a romantic relationship. Perhaps Robert is the wolf that is leading me to get off the straight path. Perhaps Dan and I would have overcome our crisis if I hadn't met Robert. Again, my thoughts run into a wall that stops me from getting anywhere.

12

I walk around the house uneasily. Even outside I don't feel free anymore. I walk hastily along the shore without noticing my surroundings. I run back into the house just as impatiently. Something is driving me. The days are slipping away from me. In six months Clifford will move back into the cottage. I wanted to have my book finished by then at the latest. For the first two months I thought it wouldn't be a problem. Now I'm not so sure anymore. I want to work but I can't. What if I can never write again? What if I feel the same way here as I did in Boston? If I sit at my desk for the rest of my days, just staring out of the window?

I wish for a miracle, a tiny miracle, one single good sentence or at least one beautiful word that will get everything moving again. In my distress I start cleaning the house. I wipe down window sills and shelves, scrub floors and clean cupboards. I make a list of activities and work it off item by item, just as if this could also eliminate the disorder inside me. The activities are the railing I hold on to while moving along; they are my protection from a dangerous abyss.

Sometimes things change by themselves in one day. But I feel a leaden standstill and don't know what would have to happen for that to change. I feel paralyzed. I am Sleeping Beauty behind the thorny hedge, after that fatal sting. Sleeping Beauty slept for a hundred years until her prince came, removed the dense undergrowth and woke her up with a tender kiss.

It shakes me up. Reluctance rises up in me, reluctance against the sticky sweetness of the images from my childhood. No, I'm not Sleeping Beauty. I don't want to wait for a prince to come and save me.

Again, I circle my desk, grope along an invisible obstacle that keeps me from sitting down, turn on the computer and continue to write. I read in my manuscript. This has helped me occasionally in the past.

The story I started only a few weeks ago seems strange to me. That surprises me, but I still like the story. I feel new confidence. Somehow I worried that it wouldn't be any good, and that would prevent me from continuing to write. That's not it. Then I noticed something else. The scene when Shirley smuggles drugs into Sarah's luggage would have been next. The drugs would be discovered by Customs, and Sarah would go to prison. In this way, Shirley would try to get rid of her competitor. All of a sudden I know that it won't work. I can't continue the story like that, not with *this* Shirley. She's much too decent for such a nasty act. I can't do it. And no reader would accept it anyway. Yet this crime was supposed to be the pinnacle of the story. I know that I can't continue writing if the heart of the story won't work.

I'm devastated. This means that I can't continue writing. It's not just a small, temporary crisis. I feel like screaming. All the work I put into this novel! How could it happen that I didn't notice this disastrous development? And yet there were warning signs that showed me that something had gotten out of hand, that my characters were moving in a completely different direction. I ignored them, and now I have to pay for it. I sit in front of my computer, torn between resignation and rebellion.

My stubbornness wins. After thirty minutes, in which I repeatedly knocked the bundle of notepads into an accurate stack, dusted the screen and thoroughly cleaned the spaces on the keyboard with cotton swabs, I turn the computer back on. I slowly scroll down the text. Where could I start? The moment Tom and Shirley become aware of their love for each other, or earlier, while they are still circling each other, unsure of each other's feelings?

I'm going back paragraph by paragraph. I reconstruct, experiment, make decisions I discard later. The story is too homogenous; I can't change it without destroying the whole fabric. I make some coffee but it doesn't taste good. I need fresh air. I suddenly notice that the air in the room is hot and stale.

I put on my coat and leave the house, almost running. Outside, I inhale the fresh, tangy autumn air. I feel relieved by the pleasant coolness on my hot forehead. The sun winks shyly through a misty veil. Where in September there was a colorful hustle and bustle almost daily, there is a wide, empty area now. Occasionally a rock, some shells, and here and there pale, bleached branches that protrude like skeletons against the sky. There's the spot where I saw the young couple just a few weeks ago – for me, they are Sarah and Tom now. The spot where they romped around like children, played like kittens and a few moments later rested in the sun. Suddenly I'm overcome by sadness. Then I defiantly decide: No matter what – I'll finish this story. The characters have come alive. Giving them up would feel like murdering them.

Suddenly a shrill scream startles me. A seagull has taken a dive close to my head. In an elegant bow, it moves on and disappears in the crowd of the other seagulls. How freely they move! I gaze at them with longing. Do the seagulls always know exactly what they're doing? Do they know their flight routes in advance? Are they really free or do they follow a set plan? I envy them for the ease their flight conveys. If only I could spread my wings and sail through the air, too!

It must be wonderful to lift up from the ground. I close my eyes, allowing myself to imagine what it might be like. I stretch out my arms longingly and turn some pirouettes. A pleasant dizziness overcomes me, and I keep spinning, faster and faster, until the world seems to revolve around me. I struggle to a halt, dizzy and feeling as if I've downed a glass of champagne too quickly. Weightless and exhilarated, I keep floating. Did the fast movements also lift a heavy load off my shoulders? I walk to the spot where the cliffs extend into the water and the beach ends. This is where I saw the naked stranger the other day. I have never gone that far since then. In my mind, I see the man, whom I had almost forgotten, standing in front of me with his wispy head of hair and the full beard, which covered almost the whole face except for his grey, penetrating eyes. A strange guy. I can't classify him. He could be the outdoor type, a bit odd, but be could also be wild, dangerous and unpredictable, maybe even insane. And then the idea comes to me, so crystal clear and self-evident that it makes me wonder why I hadn't thought of it sooner. It almost seems to me that heaven has sent me this man. Why shouldn't I let him play a part in my novel? Yes, that's exactly how the story can continue without me having to change anything at all.

Exhaling, I relax. Then I go back to the house with quick steps and get to work immediately.

13

Everything will fall into place, Grandma used to say whenever I, as a child, couldn't succeed in something despite – or *because* of – trying as hard as I could. Now I recall these words, and for the first time they make sense to me. I threw countless mosaic stones up into the air, and now they have fallen into place, creating a meaningful picture. Now the progress of the story is clear.

My fingers fly over the keyboard. Sentences drop on paper, become paragraphs and entire chapters. Hour after hour I sit at my desk. I watch the unfolding of the story with excitement. Just as I used to watch Grandma making lace, fascinated how expertly she moved the wooden cones and how a perfect pattern gradually emerged from the tangled mess of many threads.

The turmoil of the last few weeks is over. Apparently, the longed-for miracle has actually happened. My characters are now stronger and more well-rounded than I had imagined. Now they come with everything that makes them real people.

I decide not to let anything or anyone discourage me anymore. So I won't forget it, I write down these words on a small notepad and stick the note to the bottom of the screen, where I can always see it.

A competition is underway in my story. One point for Shirley, then one point for Sarah; an exchange of blows between two completely different temperaments. Shirley plays like a winner, with powerful, nimble, confident moves. Sarah seems exhausted but tough and astonishingly enduring. Occasionally her eyes seem to be pleading with me. I feel concerned. But her weakness is also her strength. It aims straight at Tom's heart.

Images appear; they haunt him. The memory of young, sweet, shy Sarah – she was fifteen when he met her – and of the blossoming, attractive, confident woman she soon became. Everyone envied him for Sarah and wondered what she saw in him – the lanky, still unfinished young man he was then. Their future plans have been shattered. In addition, their mutual friends, their families and colleagues are confused. He risked it all for Shirley, for his dream that has become real. Like a raging stream, her passion draws him along. Her impetuous vibrancy has changed him. Shirley has awaken a side of him he knew nothing about. Astonished, he suddenly feels the desire to imitate Elvis Presley or enjoys the frivolous pleasure of dancing tango with Shirley. Startled, Tom notes that his occasionally unintentionally funny and idiosyncratic step variations entertain the guests more than Shirley and Ricardo's professional dance steps. And he enjoys being the center of attention.

Suddenly there are a thousand new possibilities. Nothing has to happen, but anything is possible. Life has started to sweep him away, making him radiant. The colors around him have started to glow. Red-gold lava, dark velvet, ink blue, purple lilac, ivy green and sun yellow. »Is love doing that?« he wonders for the hundredth time, »that true love everybody is singing about, talking about?« Or are his senses simply confused? But he doesn't really want to know; he has no choice anyway.

I, too, feel gripped by a kind of suction. My sympathy oscillates between the two women. I recognize myself in the sensitive, serious Sarah and at the same time feel increasingly taken by the spirited Shirley. Curiously, I tumble through the events with my protagonists, feverishly anticipating the climax of the story with them. The end of their story will decide my own fate, too.

His appearance is inconspicuous. His hair is shorter; his eyes sparkle in an intense blue. Mr. Mitchell, the handsome new man in Sarah's life, is unmistakably the nude man from the beach. This time, however, he's smartly dressed. Sarah is captivated by him, and he, too, soon is always by her side. David Mitchell makes Sarah laugh. He is balm for her wounds. Her pain subsides. Thanks to David, Sarah becomes radiant and confident again. Her eyes glow, and her voice loses that plaintive undertone.

The new Sarah sounds challenging, almost provocative. At least that's how it appears to Tom. She walks buoyantly, signaling determination, and he thinks he can even detect a sexy swing of her hips. Is there actually a vamp inside that gentle, quiet woman that he failed to notice before, or had she put on an act in the past? Tom feels anger rising in his chest. Why is she doing this? Nobody can change just like that. Besides, this guy Mitchell isn't Sarah's type at all. In addition, she is violating the iron rule: never to start an affair with a guest. Tom comes to the conclusion: it's not real, she's just getting back at me, she wants to pay me back. A moment later, however, other unpleasant thoughts start to bother him. Will Sarah sleep with Mitchell? Will she surrender to him, to this primitive stranger, this Tarzan in designer clothes? Has she already done so? Sarah in an embrace with that stranger, not clinging and desperate as she was with him at the end, but passionate, searching, inquisitive, curious in the truest sense of the word. These thoughts nip at his flesh with sharp teeth, soon spreading over his whole body and gnawing at his smooth shell. He reluctantly shakes them off.

I try to picture what I've just written, to feel whether it is realistic. What happens when love, desire, affection, feelings that were yours until now are suddenly given to someone else? I picture Rita and Dan disappearing into the kitchen like two conspirators. Funny that they pop up in my mind right now, I hardly thought of them any more. Dan and Rita in a close embrace — what would that mean to me? I can't really envision them; they appear stiff and ungainly. Then they laugh at me, and the visions slip away from me.

Sarah feels cold for the first time since she's in this country. Is it because of the bare, gray walls that surround her or because of the shock she's still in since she was apprehended at the airport? It was supposed to be a routine operation; she had volunteered to go there because her colleague was sick. Or was there another reason? Sarah doesn't remember; she had accepted the job without thinking twice. She was just happy to be able to get away for a few days. But she didn't get far, only as far as the airport, the luggage belt she had placed her bag on and into the small room where she was checked. After that, things happened really fast. A film started, and she was suddenly in the middle of it. She's in an office, her clothes are spread out on a table, her toiletries, and in-between that little package that is totally foreign to her even though it's among all her things. People gather around her, talk to her. They keep coming back to the small inconspicuous package. They unwrap the wrapping paper and take out small plastic bags into which a brownish granulate is sealed.

»That's not mine,« she keeps insisting.

»But it's your bag – is that your bag?«

»Yes, this is my bag, but this isn't my stuff, not that package with that brown stuff in it, no ...«

A nightmare has begun, bright lights start flashing in her head, a scenario she has often heard about is taking place – right in front of her, right around her. She knows exactly what's happening here, and she can't believe it. She herself always warned the guests about this. It never happened in her environment before, and now she's in the middle of it, the leading actress.

They don't talk to her any more; they've turned away from her. They talk in a foreign language as if she were no longer there. But they talk about her, she can tell. Suddenly, her arms are brutally pulled back, handcuffs click around her wrists, distant cold faces. Mouths bark instructions, crudely, in incomprehensible foreign words, but their tone of voice is unmistakable. She is pushed to a car; then they drive through the city. The just-familiar streets are completely blurry now. She sees them through a fog – or are they tears? She doesn't cry, she doesn't want to cry, has closed down, closed her mouth and ears and even the pores in her skin. As if she was wrapped in transparent foil.

Sarah has been sitting in this gray, bleak building, a dungeon with a stone bench and a dirty mattress on it, for several hours now. She sits stiffly on what's supposed to be a bed, trying to avoid a wool blanket that is obviously soaked in dirt and sweat. She listens to steps. Everything will clear up, it's a misunderstanding or maybe it's just a bad dream. The strange noises scare her. But the silence is even worse. At least the steps tell her that she's not alone. When everything is quiet, she feels walled in, inside a tomb.

The projector in her brain throws bright images on the wall. Shirley hugs Tom, a self-satisfied smile on her face.

»She knows! Yes, she knows I'm in this jail cell.« Sarah is convinced. »She knows I'm not coming back anymore.«

New images. Shirley bends over her bag, briefly scans the room and quickly stuffs something into the bag. Sarah's imagination goes overboard.

»Of course it was Shirley! That was Shirley; she smuggled the heroin into my luggage«.

Or Shirley had somebody else do it. She pictures Shirley whispering to an airport employee, beaming at him with her seductive smile, her sparkling black eyes. He blushes, flattered and confused, then nods like in a trance. It can only have been Shirley, her inner voice keeps repeating. She wanted to force a decision. She didn't want to wait any longer. Perhaps she even feared that Tom might eventually choose her, Sarah. Yes, she did it; she wanted to eliminate her rival, who suddenly showed up, strong and self-confident, once and for all.

So where is Tom? After all, he can't just let her wither and die here. Despite everything he wouldn't do that. Not ever! Or maybe he doesn't know? Maybe he has no idea what has happened to her. Maybe no one knows. How should they? She can't remember being asked if anyone should be notified in case something happened to her. A sense of horror flows from her brain down into her body, flooding it. She begins to shiver without knowing whether she feels hot or cold. A net is spreading out over her, wire mesh cuts into her skin. What if they even planned this together, Shirley and Tom, to get her out of the way?

The high spirits Sarah was in just before this disaster now feels like mockery to her.

»Use the time while I'm away to find out what's important to you,« she said to Tom instead of goodbye. Then she walked away with firm steps, without looking back. The satisfaction she felt when seeing how irritated Tom was seems ridiculous now. His insecurity in the past few days and the sense of triumph that David Mitchell's wooing had triggered in her. Never before had she acted so resolute and so unambiguous. She felt incredibly strong. And now this crash. Pride comes before a fall. Who was it who used to say that? She can't remember but now the words haunt her.

Did I cause this drama with the way I behaved? Did I go too far, did I trigger everything myself? A thousand thoughts run through her mind. Sarah regrets everything. She'd love to undo everything. The best thing would have been not to have accepted the job in the first place. She could be in the resort right now. Entertain guests with some trivial fun and games. What a high price she will have to pay for wanting to pay Tom back!

What's at stake here is my life. My *life*. It's really at stake. Smuggling heroin – forget it, even the possession of small amounts of drugs of any kind is punishable with death in this country. Again, a shudder crawls over her skin. She almost pulls the filthy blanket over her head without thinking. But her disgust outweighs the cold. Sarah pulls the blanket away with two fingers and rolls up like an embryo that has been snatched from the womb too early. A caterpillar, carved out of the soil and now exposed to the weather without a shelter. Tormented, Sarah twists and turns before falling into a state of petrified numbness without feeling anything..

14

In Maine, winter is approaching. When I left the house a few days ago, lively little flakes were dancing through the air. This has happened more often recently, but this time it's different. It smells like snow. Now it won't be long before winter will set in. And then it happens all of a sudden. As if my thoughts had poked holes into the mountains of dense clouds in the sky, a snowstorm sets in. The snowflakes swirl through the air faster and faster, getting thicker by the minute. The wind grows stronger, and I can see hardly anything through the snow flurry. I quickly turn around and hurry back to the cabin. When I finally arrive on my doorstep again, I'm covered in a blanket of snow. The landscape has also turned white. I hang up my damp coat near the heater so it can dry. Then I watch the snowstorm from my window for a while. In here, I feel safe. The ancient heater under my feet in the basement ignites as reliable as clockwork. By now I've gotten used to the rumbling noise it makes. Through the wooden floor, it sounds like the good-natured grumbling of an old bear. In addition, I usually make a fire in the fireplace. I love the cozy crackling sound. The flames lick the wood, throwing shadows on the wall that bounce merrily. Leo spends most of the day curled up in his basket, sleeping near me. I, on the other hand, work almost without pausing to take a breath.

Tom sits across from Sarah in the visiting room of the jail. He looks at her with concerned eyes, a bit anxious and insecure. Her gaze meets his, penetrating his heart. It will haunt him for the weeks to come.

»It's his fault,« Sarah thinks, »he's the cause of what has happened.«

But while looking as at him, the pain tightens her throat. Never before has he looked so beautiful, so serious, so mature and attractive to her. He has never been so distant yet so close. Pain and resentment oscillate back and forth in Sarah's heart, growing equally strong, meeting and merging into a glowing spot.

»Sarah ...« Tom looks at her imploringly.

She swallows and looks down at her hands before starting to speak softly. »Now your new heartthrob has achieved what she intended to do: I'm out of her way.«

Tom is startled. He feels as if she slapped him in the face. »Sarah, you don't seriously believe ...«

»Well, who else is there? Who could have an interest in hurting me, getting me out of the way? And – isn't that stuff from right where she came from?«

»That stuff's everywhere and you know it,« Tom replies reassuringly and defensively at the same time.

He is shaken by the way she looks and the despair in her eyes. Sarah is pale and looks shaken. The vivacity she showed in the past weeks is gone. Now Sarah, who already lost a lot of weight recently, looks pale, fragile in the cold neon light. Her face is drawn. There are dark rings around her eyes. Her hair hangs down listlessly. She's just a shadow of her former self.

»You think I have anything to do with these drugs now, too?« She watches him warily.

»No, of course not!« He is horrified. »Sarah, no one who knows you thinks that. Don't be so desperate. Things will – *must* clear up. Trust me, I'll do everything in my power! You'll be released from this jail cell, I promise.«

Spontaneously Tom reaches for her hand, touches her delicately, caresses her trembling fingers, and for a moment they stop trembling. For a tiny moment, she is Sarah again – his girlfriend, the young, free American. For a brief moment, they are lovers again.

Then Sarah is alone again, the abandoned, the criminal among criminals, the drug smuggler, scum in a building full of scum. Removed from the society of ordinary people, a neat, tidy society.

Maybe she *did* something she shouldn't have done. Maybe she violated some law, and this is the punishment for it. She challenged fate. She played a role; she did what she used to judge others for. She acted promiscuously, proudly, almost arrogantly and boastfully. Stupid, stupid, stupid ... what an idiot she was! She sways back and forth, gets up, walks around in the confined space, closes her eyes, covers her ears with her hands until that current inside her body sounds like ocean waves. Then she lies down on the hard bunk bed and escapes into a dream, a beautiful dream full of hope. Tom will save her. He promised. He really meant it. She can still see his eyes, so warm and concerned. She could see it in his eyes. He'll do everything he can to get her out of this hell-hole. Surely he regrets the affair with Shirley now and has forgiven her for flirting with David Mitchell. This disaster will bring them back together. It is fate that's putting them to the test.

Entangled in these dreams, eyes firmly closed to keep out her horrible fear, Sarah pulls the filthy blanket over her head.

Shirley is appalled by the course the story is taking. »Karen, how could you let that happen?«

»What?« I ask, displeased about the interruption. »It's going really well right now.«

I stubbornly try to continue. Shirley's stare is reproachful. Standing in front of me, she refuses to move. Surprised, I raise my eyebrows. Will there be another argument? I thought that phase was over for good.

»You promised me I won't have to play that ungrateful part – so?«

»So what? Shirley, what're you whining about? It's Sarah who's finding herself in a bad situation – not you.«

»Sarah, Sarah, Sarah - it's always about Sarah! And even though I had nothing to do with what happened to her, everyone's blaming *me* for it!«

»Why do you think that? You and the others are not an issue right now.«

»Yeah – that's because all you care about is Sarah. I know exactly what's going on. Everybody's constantly gossiping in the whole resort, and when I show up, they stop talking.«

»They probably notice that you're miserable and are just being considerate of that.«

»Oh bull, they're not considerate of me, they never were! Don't you remember what it was like when Tom and I became lovers?«

»Yes, and I also remember that it didn't bother you at all then.«

»At the time I was fine. Today I feel awful. By now I can hardly sleep at night.« Shirley pauses. »Somehow – I don't know why – but somehow I actually feel guilty. If this goes on ... I can't work under this pressure. How am I supposed to entertain people under these circumstances?«

Her face looks distressed. Shirley really does look miserable. Her black cherry eyes fill with tears, and the corners of her mouth twitch slightly. I can't ignore her the way I intended. That's why I'm trying to reassure her. »Shirley, it's not your fault. But you're entangled in Sarah's and Tom's story, and so the events will of course affect you, too.«

»But that's not fair! I didn't want this to happen.«

»Yes, I know, but life's not always fair.« I try to sound calm and reassuring.

Shirley notices it and starts again. "But you're the one who is doing all this; you're making all the decisions, no one else does! It's in *your* power to change everything."

My gaze must have been very surprised because she suddenly pauses, terrified.

»Or don't you control the story anymore?« With widened eyes she stares at me anxiously. I don't answer. Shirley scrutinizes me sharply. I am flustered. Then I give her the only answer I can give her. I don't know if it will reassure her but at least it's honest.

»Shirley, sometimes we have to do things without knowing exactly why. But I'm sure the course of the story is just right the way it is.«

Tears start to run down her cheeks. She seems to understand that she can't change anything. We will continue along the path we've taken, no matter how difficult it may become.

When the sentences in my head start to swirl around wildly without me being able to grasp them, I leave the cottage. The snow has repainted the landscape. Even though the sky is cloudy, it's bright outside. The air is fresh and almost odorless. Instead of the autumnal rush of colors, shades of black and white dominate. Only occasionally a friendly morning or dusk covers the snow with a delicate pearly shimmer, a light blue-gray or a pale pink. Gray and grumbling, the Atlantic Ocean grinds on. It's a sluggish mass of wet cement that licks with dark tongues along the edges of the white horizon. Black trees, frozen in dance, line the beach. All life seems to have frozen under snow crystals. The landscape looks unreal and unfolds a peculiar magic.

Back at the house I discover them, footprints in the snow. They're not mine, I realize, startled. Apart from my cat, I haven't seen a living soul in a long time. The magic I just felt has disappeared in the blink of an eye. My heart starts to pound. Hypnotized, I follow the tracks that lead out of the woods, circle the house, stop in front of every window and disappear back into the woods. A curious by-passer? A forest worker? Someone from the National Park supervisory authorities? The shoe prints are large and have a concise, rough profile. I hear a snap in the thicket! Suddenly I feel as if somebody is watching me. Holding my breath, I listen and stare into the thick woods. Nothing is moving. Silence around me, nothing but cotton-like silence. All I can hear is my own breath and my pounding heart

15

This evening I lock the door especially carefully and close all the shutters on the ground floor for the first time. Then I calm down again. Nevertheless, my senses are more alert now. Most sounds have taken on a different meaning. The more I try to ignore them, the more clearly they penetrate my consciousness. Creaking wooden planks turn into stealthy steps. Even Leo's velvet paws sound heavy and plump when he sprints up or down the stairs. The cracking of a branch turns into a shot, and the fire hissing in the fireplace becomes a car that is approaching slowly.

And then there's this strange new metallic sound. It reminds me of a rattling tin bucket someone is swinging back and forth while walking. At times it sounds like a saw moving back and forth. Sometimes the sound is an even rhythm, then it falls silent for hours, so I forget it. When did it actually start?

The nocturnal sounds are particularly eerie. Muffled clanging. A snow avalanche that is falling off the roof? It might also be a snowball someone has thrown against the wall of the house. Is it somebody who wants to wake me up, wants to be let inside, needs help – or is it someone who wants to lure me out so he can attack me? The crunching sound of steps. Is he leaving again or is he just waiting for me to take a peek? In stormy nights, the wind shakes the shutters and doors. While I'm sleeping, the sounds become demons that rise from the waves rolling wildly to the shore or howling from the thicket of the frozen woods behind the house.

The next morning most of the noise has died down. The landscape looks peaceful and unspoiled. What's wrong with me? Dan warned me about loneliness. I just laughed at him and reminded him that I had often enough gone on adventure trips to remote areas. But all I knew was the loneliness of southern countries with their buzzing, rustling and chirping sounds, the familiar voices of nature. There, danger lurked when everything fell silent. This northern loneliness is different.

Although I often lack sleep, my senses are wide awake, my imagination is aroused. I spend many hours with Sarah in her bleak prison cell. The room with the small barred window is seven by ten feet in size, and the window is much too high to look out. Even when Sarah stands on the concrete bunk bed, she can get only a tiny glimpse of the blue sky. The food consists of a sticky mass in a tin bowl. I can almost taste the nasty porridge on my tongue. Sarah usually doesn't even touch it. I follow her through gloomy corridors, into moldy shower rooms with rusted fittings, where she's exposed naked to the prying eyes of other female prisoners. Beautiful, ugly, neglected, young and old faces tax her, the only white prisoner around. They talk and tattle, they muster her, try to touch her and giggle when, horrified, she tries to fend them off.

Four times a day, sometimes more often, they are allowed to walk around the prison yard. It depends on how the guard on duty is feeling that day – especially Laguna, the plump, clumsy matron with the impenetrable face, who loves to make the prisoners march in front of her. Lined up like geese, they have to pass her again and again. The guard with the feisty face watches them with narrowed eyes while the glaring sun is burning down on their unprotected heads.

The images are painful. Where do I know that pain from? The walls surrounding Sarah want to crush me, too. I can feel the heat she feels, I feel the cold, the disgusting smells – blood, sweat and urine, absorbed by the musty walls and exhaled again. I hear the groaning of those who have been forgotten, the reverberating rattle of tin, the screaming and the yelled orders. Together with Sarah, I stare up at the tiny window, desperate yet hoping, feeling the anxious stumbling of my heart. There is an oppressive memory in these images from which I extract myself with difficulty.

There have always been places I thought I knew, even though I had never visited them. One of them was Rome. I felt safe in the alleys, between the old houses with the bird-nest-like balconies and with cracks in the walls that looked like wrinkles in an old face. The Roman Forum, Colosseum, Basilica Aemilia, Via Appia; sepia-brown paintings from art catalogues, suddenly dipped in color. Quirinal, Esquilin, Pincio, Gianicolo; melodies that softly washed around my ears. I linger longingly for a moment.

After visiting Sarah, Tom is depressed and distressed. He tells Shirley nothing about Sarah's suspicions. Nevertheless, he catches himself looking at Shirley and wondering if this woman really could be capable of doing this to get rid of a female competitor.

Shirley has changed. She seems meek and insecure. Her once-delightful smile has become rare. Is this the sensitive, empathetic Shirley who is now feeling for Sarah? Does she share his guilt or is she guilty herself? He looks thoughtfully at her face. It seems sad, even now that she is bravely trying to smile. Suddenly her face reminds him of Sarah's face, and suddenly a heavy weight weighs on his chest. Does he make all the women who love him unhappy? The thought hits him in a flash and his shoulders start to sag. Sensing his despair, Shirley shyly puts her arms around his shoulders.

»What're you thinking about?« Her voice is tender and pleading, her eyes look at him anxiously. »Tom, what happened is not your fault,« she adds, trying to bridge his silence. Tom pulls away from her. Turning around, he walks over to the window and stares into the night. After a silence that seems nearly endless to Shirley, he starts to speak.

»She wanted to get away because of me, because of us. Our happiness tore her apart. In a way we *are* responsible for what happened.«

»But Tom, she was so happy in the last few weeks. You, too, thought that she wanted to go on this trip because of that guy Mitchell,« Shirley interjects.

»And that's exactly what I don't believe anymore,« Tom hisses. »You should've seen her. Then you wouldn't be so calm about it, either.«

Shirley bursts into tears. She wants to approach Tom, but after a few steps she stops with sagging shoulders.

»Tom, I can imagine that it must be horrible. I *know* it's horrible, but we're not to blame. It's a cruel mistake. You don't think … you don't really think *I* wanted this to happen?«

It's a painful cry that turns into violent sobbing. Finally Tom hugs her. »I'm sorry – no, of course I don't think that.« He burrows his face in her shoulder. Desperately, they cling to each other.

Winter has a firm grip on the country. Today is a particularly rough day. Going out takes a great effort. Storm gusts sweep dense snowflakes into my face and take away almost all of my vision. The air is damp and crawls under my clothes. I shiver even though I'm wearing my down-filled winter jacket. As soon as I step out, I want to turn around, but I need to distance myself from my story. It's the only way to escape Shirley and Sarah for at least a few minutes. And it's a necessary rest for my overheated brain. When I return to my front door after forty-five minutes, I'm glad. With clammy fingers I grope for the key in my jacket pocket. Suddenly the wind rips open the front door, rushes past me into the hallway and throws the door to the shed at the end of the hallway into its lock with a loud bang. Silence. I freeze for a few seconds. Did I forget to lock the front door? I'm confused. And why is the door to the shed open? I try to remember the last time I went to fetch some firewood. Was it yesterday or was it this morning? I can't say for sure. I pick up the key of the shed door, which fell on the floor. I put it back into the lock and turn it around twice. I recall the footprints. How crazy of me to be so reckless! I'm gripped by panic.

My heart is pounding and I hold my breath while I step into the kitchen and then walk over to the living room. Several pages of my manuscript are scattered across the floor. I feel like screaming. *Someone was here!* My heart is racing. *For sure somebody was here.*

Even my cat looks distraught.

»Was that you, Leo?« I shout at the startled animal. Thoughts of gamekeepers, weird strangers, escaped convicts and murderers running from the police buzz through my head. Following a spontaneous inspiration, I lock the door and additionally barricade it with a chair pushed under the handle. Am I about to go insane?

What if this person is still in the house? Then I can't even run away.

Thoughts of escape run through my body, but where should I run to? My hopeless situation paralyzes me. Thinking of the dusk that is already setting in, I feel trapped. I stand motionless and listen intently into the silence. Nothing moves, except for the motor of the heater that starts and stops smoothly. By now I'm totally stiff from standing still with tensed muscles. Leo has climbed back into his basket and is sleeping soundly.

»Why can't you be a dog? I could use a dog right now – not a sleepy cat.« As if Leo understood my thoughts, he opens his eyes, yawns, and goes back to sleep without a care in the world.

The storm inside my chest has just subsided somewhat when another thought starts to horrify me. What if there's someone upstairs, waiting for me? I quietly remove the chair that is stuck under the doorknob and reach for the poker next to the fireplace. In slow motion I sneak into the hallway towards the stairs. Leo seems to think I'm going to bed and happily jumps up the stairs in front of me. The plodding of his paws roar loudly in my ears. I'm horrified but don't dare to call him back.

Taking every step carefully, I follow him upstairs. Leo is obviously wondering what is keeping me so long and is happy to finally see me. It somewhat reassures me that nobody appears behind him and that his behavior is totally normal. There is no one around; otherwise I would register it in Leo's demeanor. Nevertheless I cautiously glance into every corner of the bedroom before I sit down on my bed and take a deep breath. Maybe I really did just forget to lock the door. Maybe it was only the wind that blew the pages of my manuscript onto the floor. Maybe, maybe ... It takes me forever to fall asleep.

The sun burns down relentlessly. Sweat starts to pour out of each pore of my skin. We are all sitting in a circle in the courtyard. Beefy Laguna is standing in the center, knocking two metal lids together. We're waiting for a signal but I don't know what sign. Laguna will probably change the rhythm or bang the lids together even louder. I hope I will notice the signal. I know when it comes, I will have to get up. I feel so heavy, literally stuck to the hot asphalt. What if I can't get up at the right signal? Will the others help me? I look around the circle. The others just look indifferent and jaded. No, none of them will help me. My body feels hot. There is this clanking again. Is that the signal?

I wake up, soaked in sweat, trying hard to come to my senses. My limbs are hurting. My body is feverishly hot. I hope I won't get sick. That's all I need right now. It's dark outside. I look at the alarm clock. Five o'clock. That early? I want to turn over in bed, but then I remember the horror of yesterday and am immediately wide awake. There's that sound again. For a brief moment, I picture a figure trying to open a window shutter. I quickly brush the vision aside. If I don't watch out now, I'll really go crazy.

»Get yourself together, Karen,« I tell myself. I get up and turn on all the lights. Leo comes running up the stairs; I pick him up and hold him close to me. The fact that he's okay and purring happily calms me down.

I need coffee, an invigorating shower, an aspirin just in case, and then I have to get to the bottom of that sound. This time I won't give up until I know what it is.

After it has become light outside, I dress and go outside. It is colder than yesterday, but at least it's dry. By now the sound has gone. I look up at the wall of the house but I can't see anything. Then I inspect the brackets of the shutters. They're all fixed and can't be the cause of the sound.

Damn, why isn't whatever it is knocking right now? Annoyed, I walk over to the shed. Everything is as usual. There's a car parked inside, and to its right side, some tools – shovels, rakes and a snow shovel – hang on the wall. The wood for the fireplace is stacked on the left side. An old boat that has obviously not been moved even one inch for many years is hanging in the upper part of the rear wall. There is more wood stacked up underneath it.

While standing in front of the woodpile, I suddenly hear it again, this time quite clearly. I can hear it through the door that leads from the shed to the house. But it is locked. I run out of the shed and back into the cottage. Now the sound sounds almost triumphant and it is clearly coming from the basement. I've never been down. Since I was a child, I've have been afraid of basements, these caves hidden in the ground. I feel a clear discomfort at the thought of descending into this room under my feet.

Don't go overboard, Karen. What's down there is the boiler. It has been supplying you with heat for weeks, heat you couldn't live without in this place.

I go and get the halogen lamp from the car, open the hatch in the ground and climb resolutely into the dark cave. Leo follows me excitedly and immediately disappears into the hole in the ground. I stop briefly on the wooden staircase until my eyes get used to the darkness. Then I discover a light switch. After I press it, a dim lamp lights up. Somewhat unsure of what to expect, I go down the ramshackle wooden steps.

The air is musty and moist. I turn on my halogen lamp, and immediately the dark room lights up. The beam of light glides along gray walls. Apart from the boiler, which dominates the room, I can't see much. A few old boxes; some old rusted tin buckets that might contain paint; old rags that were used for who-knows-what; a dusty sleigh, an old wooden box crammed with junk, a lobster trap and a few other devices that can no longer be identified. I jump when the motor of the burner starts to run. The sound swallows all other sounds. After a moment of panic I'm drawn deeper into the room. Masses of cobwebs suggest that no one has been here for years. I feel like an intruder in a secret room, in the very soul of the house, so to speak. I'm surrounded by the relics of other people's lives. Who might've lived here before Clifford moved in? Young people, old folks, families with children, sailors, artists, lovers and people left behind?

As suddenly as the boiler started, it stops running. The inexplicable sound that lured me down here is back. After the loud humming of the burner, it is quieter and rather unspectacular, but I finally discover its source. I can hardly believe it. Behind a grid, a tiny basement window is swinging back and forth in the breeze. Its lock is broken. Somebody had already tied the window to the frame with a string, which probably became brittle over time and was then torn apart by a storm. Completely grown over on the outside, the window is no longer visible. After I have retied the window handle, there are no more strange sounds.

Upstairs I am greeted by a bright and sunny day. Small dust particles dance through the air; there is a peaceful atmosphere around the house. Relieved, I take a deep breath. I feel better already; maybe I won't get sick after all. My limbs don't feel as heavy anymore, and the headaches are gone. Nevertheless, after this restless night, I am quite tired. I turn on the coffeemaker. While it is bubbling quietly, I sit down in the weathered brown leather armchair in the living room. Who may have sat in here and peered out at the beach?

The sun shines so intensely you might think it's hot outside. Yet in fact there is a stinging cold. I pour coffee into a cup, and after a few sips I feel refreshed and awake, taken in by this house and its former inhabitants, whose souls I can distinctly feel at this hour.

16

I love my world, my little universe. Sometimes I think I will never want to leave it again. It's a world of its own, my very own world. The protagonists are my creations. It's as if I was moving puppets on strings and things happen the way I want them to. At the same time there is this intense pull, a compulsion I can't extract myself from. I am moving in a world that has its own laws. Day, night and dream blur into one image. Excited, I move back and forth between the different levels. What's reality and what's a dream, what's true and what's fantasy? It no longer matters. The magic of this floating sensation has something seductive about it. It works like a drug. I indulge in the intensity of feelings. I'm rewarded by unlimited imagination. The glowing red of a sunset, summer lightning, storms, joy and pain. The snow is not that cold, the wind not that sharp, and my loneliness is filled with life.

»It's okay, Leo,« I quickly stroke his fur. »You'll get something to eat now.«

I fill his bowl. Eating and sleeping seem to be his main activities right now. I, on the other hand, sometimes forget my basic needs until my trembling hands, a queasy feeling in my stomach or Leo remind me of them. My rhythm of life has been changing continuously. I often write until the late hours just to wake up after only a few hours. At other times I fall asleep from one moment to the next, sleeping so deeply for half an hour as if I were dead. I'm constantly looking for things, such as my keys, and at times end up with a pale yellow brew instead of coffee because I forgot to put coffee into the filter. Such carelessness is rare for me. Now it occurs more and more often. But it seems to me that these are banalities compared to what's emerging right now. A new world, a cosmos created by me, fireworks of images, voices and sounds. Only a stovetop that is already glowing because I forgot to turn it off reminds me of the dangers this complete immersion into my story carries with it. In these moments I urge myself to pay more attention.

»Karen, how long do I have to stay in this prison cell? I can't stand it anymore.« Dressed in her thin dress, Sarah stumbles miserably through the sand next to me. I can't believe it – now I can't even have a peaceful minute here at the beach.

»Sarah, you'll catch a cold. Let's talk about it when we get home,« I say reluctantly. She just stares at me, dumbfounded. Her face is reddened but she doesn't seem to feel the cold.

»Karen, why don't you want to say anything? Are you thinking about letting me die?« She steps in front of me, blocking my path. »Tell me what will happen, will you?«

I'm getting angry: »What're you talking about? What good would that do?«

Sarah has planted herself in front of me in anger. »Maybe so that your darling Shirley will have free rein?« Her voice is full of mockery now.

»Darling, darling! What nonsense!« I reply angrily, pushing her aside and moving on resolutely. She stays on my heels. The fact that she's running next to me makes me nervous. I try to walk faster to get rid of her, but she follows me as light-footedly as a feather.

»Now you're not saying anything anymore.« Her eyes sparkle furiously. »How can you like her? She took Tom away from me, and she's also to blame for everything else. Everything!« Her voice has taken on a shrill tone.

»Sarah, Tom wanted it, too. A relationship always involves two.«
»She seduced him.«
»Sarah!«

Just as I fled outside, I rush back to the house and my desk. Again, my manuscript is messed up. What does it mean? Somebody has created a pattern made of shells on the page on top. It looks like something Shirley would do. These are small messages that should not be overlooked. I find them everywhere. Full glasses, several used coffee cups, and manuscript sheets everywhere. The other day there was even something scribbled on it, which I couldn't decipher, however.

»What's the purpose of this anyway?«

Suddenly I spot puddles of water on the ground.

»Who poured something out here?« I shout into the room in a shrill voice. Now they are silent. Of course right now they stick together. I feel a grumbling rising in my chest. And panic. I am sitting on a violently rocking raft and fear I might fall into the water any moment. I quickly suppress the unpleasant feeling.

»I know you guys did this.«

There are footprints. Footprints? A sudden fright grips me. Then I look at my feet.

»Oh, sorry, it was probably me.« I take off my shoes and put them in front of the heater so they can dry. Then I wipe up the water on the floor. No, I don't want to get upset about such little things anymore. I put the shells back on the window sill. Tomorrow they may be somewhere else. It's probably a game, a game whose rules I don't understand.

Sarah hears steps in the hallway and the clattering of keys. In front of which door will they stop? She listens anxiously. She is afraid of these sounds yet longingly waiting for them. They could mean anything. A message, mail, an interrogation, in any case that something is happening. The steps fall silent behind her door. The key is inserted into the lock and turned over. Expectantly, she looks up. It is one of the guards. He asks her to come with him. He says a word that probably means a visit. Tom? Is it Tom? Her heart takes a joyous little leap. But then they pass the visitor room and keep going. Their steps reverberate in the bare corridors, which seen to stretch endlessly. Finally, they enter a small room that is unfurnished except for a table and some chairs. Tom is actually there, waiting for her. But he is not alone. Impatiently, he rushes towards Sarah.

»Sarah, that's Rafin Hamid, your attorney.«

The man he introduces to her is small and slender. He is dressed in a formal suit and his face registers no emotion. He greets her with a short nod.

»Sarah, he will help you. He's the best attorney I could find for a case like yours.«

No! Her inner voice is screaming, not him. But how could she tell Tom that in the attorney's presence? Tell him that she doesn't like this wiry little man, that she has no confidence in him and that it seems impossible to her to put her fate into his hands?

»Will he be able to understand me?« she asks Tom, hoping for a moment he'll say that they will unfortunately need an interpreter. Tom assures her enthusiastically that Rafin Hamid had studied in the U.S. for a few years, speaks perfect English and specializes in cases like this. If Hamid didn't understand her, she could ask Tom to look for another, perhaps an American attorney – instead of him, who looks like the very people who arrested her, who are holding her captive, constantly watching her with nasty glances.

I don't want him, I don't want him, her inner voice is screaming. She wants to throw herself at Tom's chest. She desperately longs for his embrace, especially now that he is so close to her. Usually there are security guards around, so they have to sit across from each other and only their hands can touch. Now she's standing in front of him as if petrified. The attorney to whom she owes this unguarded meeting is keeping her from hugging Tom by simply being there. So Sarah finally lets herself be led to the table like a doll and sits down across from Rafin Hamid without wanting to. He actually speaks perfect American English, explaining objectively and soberly the approach he will take and the next steps. Sarah listens in silence. She will receive a full translation of the indictment in the coming days. She should read it and tell him the facts from her point of view. It is a small consolation because at least something is finally happening.

Sarah can't get used to this impersonal man who is now supposed to be responsible for her fate. On another visit Tom can finally convince her that Hamid, despite his unapproachable nature, is the right legal representative for her.

»Sarah, you need a lawyer who knows not only the laws but also the mentality of the people here. Rafin Hamid also has the best connections. What good is it if you like someone but if he can't help you?«

Sarah feels handed on to Hamid by Tom. However, she must admit that the lawyer has obtained some fast relief for her. The food is a little better. Occasionally she finds quite familiar things on her tray. Bread, cold cuts and cheese, fruit and vegetables. She has also gotten some pens and paper and hungrily devoured some books in English. Reading the indictment, on the other hand, becomes an ordeal. Sarah's mood alternates between boiling anger and resigned apathy. She mentally goes through the day she was apprehended, the hours before and after her arrest. Her triumphant farewell to Tom, the last yards to the luggage check. She can still feel how she was brutally grabbed on the arm and dragged into that small office. She sees the open travel bag, her clothes spread out on the table and the small package in between her travel items. She sees mouths with white teeth that keep moving, hears voices that yell at her. She feels how her arms are brutally pulled back and how handcuffs click around her wrists. They could tell that she was guilty. She allegedly confirmed that the items on the table belonged to her. One monstrosity follows the other for many pages. Her words were twisted, distorted, so that they sounded like admissions of guilt. With an outraged heart, Sarah comments on each sentence, each point, without paying attention to her fingers, which will soon be raw.

I can no longer sit calmly at my desk, and the concentration is also becoming increasingly difficult for me. My brain refuses to come up with even one more sentence. I look at the clock. No wonder, I have been working for five hours without a break. My body demands movement and fresh air. Outside, I'm greeted with snow. Flakes swirl into my hot face, melt on my cheeks and slowly fall down. I have to force myself to walk on. I pull the hood of my winter jacket deeper into my face and wrap my scarf tightly around it so that it won't slip off. I can see only a few feet ahead of me. Yet to my surprise there is somebody on the beach, a figure wrapped in a coat and scarf who walks away with quick steps. It reminds me of the footprints around my house that scared me so much. I briefly consider whether I should hurry up to the person and address him. But then I discard the idea. What should I say to him?

»Did you sneak around my house the other day? What do you want from me?«

It seems impossible to ask. Moreover, the stranger – I'm sure it's a male – has pulled up his shoulders and doesn't seem to take any notice of his environment. Strange that the man who had telephoned for me in Bath never called again.

Suddenly he appears in front of me: Mitchell, in a deep tan and dressed in summer clothes. I'm startled; I want to turn around and leave. But he's blocking my way. At least this time he's not nude. His eyes are as piercing as they were then.

»Listen to me,« he says in a soft, haunting voice, »did you think you could just put me in a book and get rid of me?«

»What do you want from me?« I ask, frightened and startled.

»I want to warn you ...«

»But –« Before I can ask him what about, he's gone again.

Irritated, I go back to the house. Only when I've reached the doorstep, do I dare to turn around. He's gone.

Uneasy, I open the door. I'm welcomed by a fragrance, very subtle, only a hint and yet perceptible. Is it perfume or aftershave?

As I rummage through my memory to see where I smelled it before, I go into the living room. On the table, everything is unchanged. The screen is on. Actually, I'm sure I turned it off. As I ponder, my gaze falls on what was last written. What is that? I can't believe what I'm reading.

» ... and you had no concerns, no suspicion? Hasn't he contacted you since then? No?«

My eyes read on in horror.

»It's always the same approach. He gains your trust, friendship, love — then he destroys you.«

Have I gone crazy? I never wrote that; it's completely changed. Shocked, I read on.

»He was always here,« he whispers.

»Karen feels uncomfortable.«

Karen? I'm grabbed by fear.

»His face did not reveal anything even though he had almost read all of her notes. Then he pushed the stack of paper aside and looked at it.«

I suddenly feel the presence of someone else in the room. A shudder creeps over my back. Abruptly I turn around but I can't see anyone. I listen. Then I stare back at the unknown text.

»What changed in your life before the event?«

»I had an argument with my partner.«

»Were there any other people in your life?«

»No.«

»He didn't come back, but he's always been here ...«

In a panic, I print out the pages I have just read and a few moments later I see the mysterious, incomprehensible words in black and white in front of me. My head is spinning.

»It's a software virus! Or maybe Sarah and Shirley –? But maybe I've ... No, I don't have an answer.«

»Did *you* do that?« I scream into the silent room. »Come out, talk to me!« My heart is beating wildly.

»Calm down, Karen, relax, don't go crazy!« But I can't expel the horror I feel. It sits in front of me like a hungry animal that demands its food.

»Mitchell, it was Mitchell,« I whisper to myself. »He threatened me.«

Surprised, Leo looks at me; he gets up and circles my legs soothingly. I pet him, lost in thought. Whose fragrance was that? Helplessly, I stand in the room. Then another scary thought shakes me up. My book, my whole book, what if more text has been changed, what if none of it is right anymore? The floppy disk! I'm sure I saved the text before I left the house. A rou-tine habit of mine since a thunderstorm let my computer crash and I lost an almost finished article. I save the strangely altered text under a different name and reload the novel text from the flop-py disk. I open it, and it's there as if nothing had happened. Un-changed, just the way I remember it all. I take a deep breath. I've started to sweat, and my mouth is totally dry. I take off my damp jacket and gulp down a glass of water. Then I review the scene with the meeting between Sarah and her lawyer: Rafin Hamid reads through her notes. Sarah feels uncomfortable. His face betrays nothing. She would have preferred to get up and walk around the room but she doesn't dare to. So she alternately stares at her hands and his face. His glasses have slipped down to the tip of his nose. His face reveals nothing. Finally, he raises his head, pushes the stack of paper away and looks at her.

»It may all be true the way you wrote it down, but somehow the heroin got into your luggage.«

Sarah almost stops her breath. »But what I wrote is the truth. Don't you believe me?«

»It doesn't matter whether I believe you or not. That won't help us.«

»I don't know how that stuff got into my luggage. Somebody must've put it there!« Sarah almost screams. Tears run down her cheeks. If her own lawyer doesn't trust her, who else will?

»What changed in your life immediately before the event?« he inquires soberly.

»I had an argument with my partner, with Tom,« she replies softly. »He has a relationship with another woman.«

But Rafin Hamid is not interested in that. »And apart from him – were there any other new people in your life?«

»I became friends with a man.«

»How did you meet him?«

»He was one of the guests,« she whispers. She feels as if she's on trial.

»How did he approach you?«

»I was unhappy, he was attentive and charming. He comforted me.«

»And you had no concerns, no suspicions?«

Sarah is startled. »You think he –?«

»Has he been in contact with you since then?«

»How should he know where I am?«

»You think he doesn't know that you weren't on the plane?« When she doesn't answer him, he speaks. »It's always the same approach. They gain somebody's trust, friendship, affection – and in your situation that was particularly easy – and then they use that person for their operations. With you, the risk seemed to be particularly low to him. Presumably, he didn't expect a tour guide to be checked as thoroughly as the other passengers.«

Sarah is devastated. She can't, no, she *doesn't* want to believe it. One man has cheated on her, and the other one has supposedly used her.

I am relieved. The text about Sarah's conversation with her lawyer has not been changed, but my uneasiness remains and I feel strangely exhausted. It's impossible for me to continue with the story today. I decide to revise previous chapters and manage to distract myself. While dusk settles in, my unrest increases. How will I make it through the night? I feel like hiding under my blanket. But there the ghosts attack me even more unbridled. I wish I had a radio or a television. None of my books can captivate me. Full of desperation, I take Leo, who is sleeping, out of the basket and, like in the old days, bury my face in the fur of my startled cat.

»Stay with me, I need you now!«

A bit reluctant and with flattened ears, he gives in to my tight embrace. Nervously I walk back and forth between the living room and the kitchen. Then I remember the bottle of wine. Yes, that's my salvation! I purchased that special wine for a possible visit from Robert. I let my relieved cat go; he shakes himself briefly and immediately climbs back into his basket. I retrieve the bottle from the farthest corner of the kitchen cupboard. Still in the kitchen, I fill a glass with the dark red liquid and immediately take a big sip. In a matter of seconds I feel the alcohol spreading warmly into every limb – I haven't taken a sip of alcohol for several weeks. Armed with the bottle and my glass, I settle down in the brown leather armchair, listen to the blazing fire and observe the shadows on the wall. At some point, I go to bed, feeling comforted and indifferent.

The next morning I feel rather beaten. I have a light headache. It takes me some time to decide to get up. Only the view out the window encourages me a little. It has finally stopped snowing. Finally a day that is not gray. Now a cup of coffee; it might just become a rather decent day.

»Yes, Leo, I'm coming. Now get out of my way.«

In his joy to see me, he keeps blocking my way. I feed the starved cat and turn on the coffeemaker before taking a shower. After breakfast, it takes some time before I can decide to turn on the computer. What if something has been changed again? After I have gathered the courage to check a short passage, I am reassured. Everything looks unchanged. I start to focus on the text.

Sarah is sitting on the mattress, staring into a bleak distance. Today, she can't read or write down what she feels. It's as if she's used up all of her energy in the last few weeks. She squandered it, wasted it, everything was in vain. She constantly grabs her neck, trying to remove the rope she feels at her throat. Even more horrible are the images of a knife or a heavy axe. She feels the sharp pain of a slash, feels the pounding of her heart and sees a flowing stream of blood swelling from the wound. She remembers the hair-fine cut of a sheet of paper and the burning sensation. There was no blood seeping out of that wound, but it burned like fire nevertheless. How would it feel? What is it like when a knife separates the head from the body? Is the pain over quickly?

The morning of the trial has come. Sarah, the sacrificial lamb. She sees the crowds in the courtroom, feels the excited and cheerful mood of the spectators. When the process begins, every seat is taken. It is stuffy in the room, and in no time the air becomes so thick you could cut it. That doesn't seem to bother anyone but her. Would these people witness her execution just as cheerfully? She feels sick, feels as if she's choking. Struggling against that sensation, Sarah takes deep breaths. The air feels like poison. It will kill me, she thinks. But maybe she will just sink to the floor in the next few minutes. Sweat trickles down her body. How will the crowd react if she, the leading actress of the play, faints and drops to the ground? If the spectators are deprived of the show they are awaiting so eagerly. The murmur of voices reminds her of the audience in a theater before the curtain opens.

Still, she keeps on hoping in desperation. After all, she has been looking forward to this day for weeks. She was so sure that it would bring her a great deal closer to freedom. She wanted to look decent today and so she had Tom bring her one of her dresses. The blue linen dress feels strange and loose on her body.

On the way to the courthouse, her memories blaze like fire. It is almost the same route as the one on the day of her arrest. Countless cars and people move through the streets in a colorful mix. In the city, life has gone on as if nothing happened. That's exactly how it started, she thinks, and maybe it will end that way. Freedom is so close, only separated from her by a car window. At this moment she even dares to hope for a small miracle; maybe she will be free by the end of the day.

But then everything turns out differently. The judge and the prosecutor enter the room and, in their black robes and white curly wigs, reinforce the feeling of being in the middle of a theater performance. The murmur subsides; the mood around her changes. The prosecutor and the judge say something, the trial starts. Personal data is mentioned, Sarah recognizes her strangely pronounced name. The charges are read. The interpreter hisses sentences at her, interrupting her concentration. She breathlessly follows their glances and gestures, hoping she will be able to speak soon, that she will finally be heard. Words push themselves into her consciousness, fill her throat, chest, her whole body, every cavity, burn on her lips. But her lawyer stops her with a small, unequivocal gesture. Startled, Sarah pauses. He says something, calm and impersonal, sober and matter-of-fact.

What did the interpreter say? Sarah is irritated by the tangle of languages. She no longer understands anything. Apparently it is about her arrest.

Why doesn't he say that part about Mitchell she wonders. Again, she looks at her lawyer inquiringly. He doesn't register it. His face is unchanged. She doesn't seem to matter at all, as if she were not even there. It is just like when she was arrested. They are talking about her but not *with* her. What is it all about? Is no one here interested in the truth? Is it all just a game, a show, a sham trial? What's being played here? She doesn't understand the rules. Her lawyer's strategy is also not clear to her. A dispassionate struggle. Why doesn't he fight for her? Isn't he on her side? Or has the outcome of the trial been fixed from the outset? Sarah's outrage collapses, making way for great despair. She looks helplessly around herself. In the crowds she discovers a familiar face: Tom! He, too, looks anxious. He has come alone, of course; now he is finally taking her feelings into consideration. This realization does not fill Sarah with joy or triumph. Instead she only feels a great emptiness. No, no miracle will happen today.

To this day, her rage has sustained her, her outrage at the injustice. She saw herself as the leading actress of a drama, and Tom's feelings of guilt felt good. She felt sorry for herself because of the bad food, the cold and the heat, the moldy shower rooms, her small prison cell and her depleted, tender body. Worst of all, however, was the loss of individuality and freedom. In a single day, everything has changed. The possibility of moving from this gray building to death row in a short time suddenly appears like a real threat.

So what's the point of Tom suffering, even when his affair with Shirley will be over because of this? The narcissistic pain and insult to her vanity become ridiculously childish, considering the possibility of being dead soon. The idea that her breath would no longer lift and lower her chest, her body, abruptly separated from the thread of life, would remain silent. The decomposition of her body would begin, and ultimately her lifeless shell would be thrown away like a worn dress. Her existence would be destroyed and ended so soon and willfully, before she had really begun to live. She would never see snow again, never her parents, grandparents and friends again, no more spring flowers, no roses, no more trees and meadows. Not even that little piece of blue sky she can see from her cell. How precious it seems to her now. She is shaken by deep despair.

She wants to live, to live, to live ... Nothing else matters more than living, continuing to breathe, not being killed. Continuing to live without Tom. Tom no longer matters, neither does Shirley, her profession, her career, money, fashion and clothes, a nice house. Why did she get so upset because of Tom's affair with

Shirley? Why did she think the world would stop turning? What did she know about real tragedy? Life, now that it is suspended merely on a thin thread, how incomparably precious it is at this moment. Just to live – if need be, for weeks, months or even years in this cell. She must live, even with the slightest hope of freedom, at some point. Twenty, thirty, forty, fifty, maybe even sixty years of her life. Yes, it's worth fighting for. As long as she's alive, she has a chance. A chance for freedom, a chance that the door will open again for her one day, that she will step out into the street, immerse herself in the stream of people, breathe fresh air, feel the sun or fresh sparkling rain. Hear voices, laughter, smell the flowers, see the lakes and rivers, walk on a forest path, listen to music. Yes, that's happiness, perfect immeasurable happiness, true wealth.

The longing, the longing and the grief for unlived possibilities almost tear her apart. But in some hidden corner of her heart, hope germinates, new and powerful.

17

After another thirty minutes of work, I feel exhausted and empty. Today I am content with my workload and I have to escape the sad images for an hour. I enjoy the opportunity to be able to do just that. Freedom is the most valuable asset there is. I carefully save my text on the floppy disk and put it in the box next to the computer. But suddenly I have doubts. Spontaneously I save the text on another floppy disk, put the disk in an envelope and hide it in my closet. Somewhat relaxed, I then leave the house. The fresh air feels good. Hopefully my protagonists will stay in the house today. I don't want to argue with them. I don't want to talk to anyone at all. I just want to walk, move, listen to the sound of the waves. Feel the wind and perhaps follow the seagulls with my eyes, watch their unfathomable curves and arches. Let things happen and simply be.

Although it doesn't snow, it's unpleasantly chilly. Automatically I step up the pace while I mentally return to Sarah's trial. Couldn't there be a decision made at the next court date? The grueling process torments me. The bow is drawn. How far can, must, should I go? One inch, then one more, and another one? When will the arrow fly? Well, I'll find out. Impatience would only spoil everything. It would be like picking an unripe fruit. I have to proceed with care, otherwise I will destroy everything.

When I get back to the cottage, I first storm into the living room because of what happened last time, checking the room. The screen of my computer is off. My manuscript is still sitting in the same place and looks untouched. I am reassured and decide to make coffee before I continue working. In the kitchen, my gaze immediately falls on the table. A bottle of wine is sitting there, a glass, and next to it a dark rose in the water-filled wine bottle I finished off yesterday.

Drink to our freedom with me, is written on a piece of paper. I suddenly feel dizzy; my knees go soft. I sink into a chair, afraid that the floor will open up and devour me the next moment. I quickly remove the cork, which is already loose, fill the wine glass and hastily gulp it down. The wine is delicious. It is a dry, black shimmering red wine. While drinking, I can taste the grapes on my tongue. I swallow. My mouth becomes dry, with coated tongue, and I notice a bittersweet aftertaste.

The long-stemmed rose is also nearly black. I touch it to check if it's real. It is quite velvety and definitely genuine. I should eat something, I think. Suddenly the scenario starts to blur before my eyes.

»Drink to our freedom with me! What does that mean?« I ask with a heavy tongue, addressing the empty kitchen.

»I'm Karen, I'm not Sarah. I'm not locked up. Karen, you are the only author in the world whose characters have actually come to life,« I slur to myself. The room is spinning. Delicate sounds set in, swell, cheerful exuberant music. Sarah and Shirley dance in front of me. They laugh at me, ask me to dance with them. I want to approach them, touch them, but my knees are shaking. Then someone pushes me back to the chair. Is it Tom?

»Stay here; don't leave me.« He hands me another glass of wine. »Drink, Karen, drink. This is our party.«

He puts the glass to my lips and smiles. I want to push it away. Now it's no longer Tom, it's Robert smiling at me. Fascinated I look into the face that is so close to me.

»Drink, Darling,« he whispers. What kind of a voice is that? It sounds quite hoarse and tender. Sarah and Shirley laugh.

»What are they laughing about?«

»They are happy for us.«

»Why?«

»Because soon nothing will separate us any more.«

A feeling of happiness spreads through my veins. I think I'm dancing. No, I'm not dancing. I'm floating. The walls revolve around me, I see blurry faces. I feel weightless; I think I'm floating under the ceiling. Then a vortex opens up in front of me, greedily sucking me into it.

The dark night surrounds me. Where am I? I glance at the luminous dial of the alarm clock. It's right before five a.m. How did I get into bed? I grope for the light switch. Startled, I close my eyes, blinded by the brightness. My ears are roaring, I feel hot, the air smells stale. My bed is a mess. A faint memory creeps into my consciousness. That was a strange dream! Or wasn't it a dream at all? A frightening thought makes me freeze. What happened? Abruptly, I sit up. My clothes are scattered across the floor. I am naked. I feel nauseous; my skull is buzzing. I want to jump up and open the window. My body doesn't obey me; the whole room seems to sway. I'm staying in bed, hoping the dizziness will subside soon. While I'm waiting with closed eyes, I try to figure out the events of the last few hours. A dull thumping sound startles me.

18

Leo has jumped on my bed and is now walking all over me. Tired, I ruffle his fur.

»Can you tell me what happened?«

He purrs; he's probably hungry. I feel like I will never again be able to get up.

Coffee, I need coffee. No, tea! Tea is better, my stomach tells me. But first a shower. I force myself to get up, drape my bathrobe over my shoulders. Oh my God, what did I drink last night — and how much? I remember the bottle of wine. What bottle of wine *was* that? I didn't have any left. Blurred images flicker, memories of dance and music, a voice whispering into my ear. Was there really anyone there? I have to check immediately what it looks like in the living room and kitchen.

With slightly unsure steps I climb down the stairs. Leo follows me happily. There is nothing unusual in the kitchen — on the contrary, everything is tidy. Where's the bottle, the glass? I check the living room. There, too, everything looks untouched. The heater is buzzing peacefully as always. The computer is turned off. The manuscript is a neat stack. Everything looks as if nothing out of the ordinary happened yesterday afternoon and evening.

Now I've really gone mad, I think.

The note, there was a note with a message. I look in the garbage can. Nothing — neither a piece of paper nor a bottle nor anything else that would confirm last night's events, which are a nebulous memory. Was it just a dream? But why do I feel so bad then? Rather confused, I walk back and forth between the rooms several times; then I step into the shower. For several minutes I let the water run over my head and body. First warm, then cold, then warm and cold again. At last I feel a little better. I dry myself, rub my hair dry with a towel, wrap myself into my bathrobe and go downstairs.

Sarah sits motionless on her bed, with bent knees and closed eyes. Her face is pale and relaxed, as if she has distanced herself from the world. In fact she no longer notices her environment. She has discovered a way to escape her prison at least for a while. Sarah listens to herself, listens to her heartbeat, this pounding that quickly calms down. Soon her heartbeat is accompanied by delicate sounds. It is easy for her to leave this prison cell; her thoughts have simply floated out, walls can't stop them. Now she is sitting on a lush green spring meadow, a warm breeze caresses her cheeks, and she inhales the scent of flowers and grass. Her sense of heaviness has fallen from her. Her body is light. Or is she no longer inside her body? Faces appear, friendly, familiar faces. Sarah recognizes her parents, her grandparents and friends. They wave at her with a smile. They seem to be very close, but she can't touch them, even talk to them. Is this what dying feels like? A jerk goes through her body. Is what she's doing here a good idea or is she going mad now? Removed from the place where she no longer wants to be. It scares Sarah; she pulls herself together. What if one day she can't find her way back?

Suddenly I feel nauseated. I definitely need to eat something. Of course – it's been about sixteen or eighteen hours since my last meal. I've been forgetting to eat more often lately. Even now I'm not hungry, but I know I have to force myself to eat. With trembling hands, I cut a slice off a loaf of bread and spread butter on it. I force it down with some tea but I still don't feel any better. I break out in small beads of sweat; I must lie down quickly. So I go to the bedroom, armed with a cup of tea. I climb over the heap of clothes lying on the floor, open the window and drop down on my bed. Soon thereafter my whole body starts to shiver. I wrap myself tightly into my blanket. I worry about getting seriously sick. »I'll have to take better care of myself,« I mumble to myself before falling asleep.

When I wake up again, it's bright daylight. It is cold in my bedroom. I'm freezing, but I feel better. I close the window, dry my hair, which is cold and moist, with the hair-dryer. I will go for a walk, have a long breakfast and then continue working.

Before I leave the house, I make extensive arrangements. I save my text and secure it on the floppy disk next to the workstation. I tuck a second backup disk into the pocket of my jacket. Then I check if the windows and the door to the shed are locked. I make sure there are no glasses and cups around and the computer is turned off. Only then do I leave the house, somewhat reassured.

Tiny snowflakes swirl through the air, and the air is frosty. I wrap myself into my jacket. Indifference and resignation pull me down; it seems to me that I have been looking at the same scenery for months: a dreary, dead gray. For the first time I feel the desire to leave. Walking away from this cold, the loneliness, this bleak gray and the strange things that keep happening to me. With all my heart I long for the sun, warm weather and people around me. To put my suitcases in my car and drive away, to Grace, to my parents or to my cheerful, practical grandmother. She would certainly encourage me, she always did. I could hide there for a while and at some point start to do something else. But while this thought is still warming my heart, I know I can't do it. Countless tiny shackles are holding me back. It would be an escape, no, it would be worse, it would be as if my life was suddenly going backwards. The last few years would be in vain. I may not get another chance because I have exhausted all the opportunities anyone gets in life. I fear Sarah, Shirley and Tom will have to stay here forever. I could never finish my book or start a new one.

I arrive at the rocks. This is where I met Mitchell. Today I see only rugged and repellent boulders where the water breaks before it rolls back into infinity. Where might he be right now? Just don't think of him, otherwise you might summon him up. I haste back to the house.

What will await me inside? No, don't think about it, or else something *will* happen. I'm scared of my own thoughts; they appear unwanted, I don't have any control over them. And they have so much effect. I walk faster and faster, the closer I get to the house. Nervousness envelops me. Unexpectedly Leo comes to meet me. At first I'm just surprised. His tail is puffed up and vibrates. His whole body expresses irritation. Anxiously, he walks in circles around my legs. Then shock sets in. He was inside the house, he wasn't outside at all! It's impossible for him to be out here!

I know for sure now that something bad has happened or is about to happen. Dizziness overcomes me; my knees start to buckle. My heart races. I want to stop moving yet I move on. My mouth is dry, the nausea is back. My thoughts are racing. There's a whirlwind in my brain. I can feel a headache coming. I can't stop anything from happening anymore. While I approach the house as if controlled by an unknown power, I keep talking to Leo. Talking is the only valve I have left.

»What're you doing here, how did you get out?« My voice sounds hysterical. I keep thinking: Now it's time, now it's going to happen. Someone will be there. Sarah and Shirley. I gave them too much life, too much power. They have taken control of the story and the house. Or Mitchell is there, that nude man, who is warming up inside with that insane look on his face.

As I approach the door, turn the knob, and the door opens without any resistance, even though I had closed it, I am desperately looking for another option. It can't be like this, it simply can't. There must be an explanation for all this. It's surely quite harmless. Maybe everything turns out to be a nice surprise. Crazy thoughts overcome me. Robert will be sitting in the living room, enjoying his successful prank. Or Clifford has come by for a visit. Or Grace or somebody else I just can't think of now. Any second now I will break out in relieved laughter. I picture myself telling this unusual story later, and everyone will be amused. I think of the little scorpion I found in my bed on one of my trips to Africa. Or the lions who sneaked around my tent on a safari tour. Once I felt as if someone was following me in a city, but it was only the waiter who was carrying my notebook, which I had left behind. All the horrors I had imagined back then while I was running ... Everything has always gone well.

I think all this as I enter the quiet house. How much you can think in a few seconds! I hear the loud creaking of my careful steps on the wooden planks and am horrified. My own breath sounds like a loud wheezing to me. Even the crackling of my winter jacket was never this loud before. In the living room, the cursor of the blue screen flashes at my workplace. There is a note in front of it.

E N D – No one but me will ever own you again.

19

All my text is deleted. I am horrified. No, this is not a joke. Someone is playing a sick game with me. In the kitchen there is another bottle of wine on the table, a glass is sitting next to it. Dark red petals are scattered across the table. Now I can also remember again, not everything, but many images. The wine, the rose, a message, the intoxicating effect the first glass already had, voices, music. A man and his tender words. The rest of the night is deleted in my memory. Suddenly, for a tiny second, a shadow appears in the square of the kitchen window. That's him! He's watching me! He wants to see what I will do!

Crazed, I run out of the house and around it. No, I'm not crazy, I haven't been this sober for a long time. I follow the footsteps and run after a dark figure that is hurrying away. Branches crackle and snap. A car door slams, an engine roars. Taillights light up and disappear fast in the distance.

I can picture everything. No, I'm not crazy. Now I know better. That fact is both a relief and a shock. There was someone here; it was all staged, it was not my imagination. All that has happened in the last few weeks has not been some fantasy. Somebody actually did go in and out of this house as he pleased. That person has a key. He was able to get in, even though all the windows and doors were locked.

With every second I become more aware of the enormity of this realization. He could have come into the house at night while I was sleeping. Or in the morning, while I was in the shower and then went into the kitchen, dressed only in a bathrobe. He could have walked up behind me while I was concentrating on Sarah and Shirley. He could have robbed me and forced me to do anything. He could have hurt me or even killed me.

He didn't. He? I'm sure it's a man. What, for God's sake, does he want from me? The incomprehensible monstrosity of it all is horrifying. I go back inside the house. The caller, that mysterious caller, must have been him. He never called again; instead he got the key. He took it off the hook in an unnoticed moment when he was at Grace's and then he started to look for me. That's exactly how it must have been.

Slowly I struggle through the snowstorm to Bath. Although it is only four p.m., the countryside is already fallen into impenetrable twilight. My car is the only car on the road. Only a crazy person would be on the road right now – or someone in my situation. The ground is extremely slippery. I need to focus on the road. Just don't get off the road, don't step on the brakes. Maybe he's hiding somewhere, watching me. My whole body is soaked in sweat. The ride, for which I normally only need forty-five minutes, takes more than two hours. When I finally get to Bath, I feel incredibly relieved.

Grace is surprised to see me, especially in this weather. But she registers at first glance that something extraordinary must have happened to me.

»Karen, what is it, what makes you come here in this weather?« She asks me, startled, and looks at me questioning.

»Grace, is the key to my house still there?« I say frantically without even saying hello. »Somebody has been coming inside.«

»Calm down, Karen! What happened?« She gently pulls me into her office and takes me to the only chair that is not covered with some documents. She clears a second one for herself and sits down across from me. »Now tell me.«

Extremely confused, I tell her about the events and observations I made during the past few weeks. Grace listens to me earnestly and concerned. Then she disappears into the kitchen, but she returns immediately.

»Well, the key is still hanging where I put it.«

»Then he had a copy made,« I say excitedly.

»Karen, who would do such a thing?«

»The mysterious man who called here and asked for me.«

»That's impossible,« Grace says, shaking her head. »There's always somebody here. A stranger would have been noticed. And why should anyone do something like that?«

Grace doesn't believe me, and even Harry, who has appeared behind her, looks at me doubtfully. Or isn't that more of a sly glance? Is he possibly involved in these mysterious occurrences?

»Maybe it's no stranger,« I answer softly. Even while I am uttering it, I become aware of the monstrosity of my claim. I really have to be careful so I won't start to suspect everybody soon.

Grace shakes her head again. »No, that doesn't make sense. Why would someone drive to your house every day, check out the rooms, do weird things to you, and then disappear again?«

»Maybe a voyeur who enjoys scaring women. Or somebody who wants to drive me crazy,« I quietly respond even though I know it sounds totally insane.

Grace sits across from me, looking at my face without saying anything. Suddenly she caresses my cheek. It's a delicate gesture that is extremely unusual for Grace. As if this shocked even her she clumsily grabs my right hand. It feels warm and secure between her hands while her eyes scan my face.

»Karen, you look exhausted – maybe you've been working too much lately?«

»That, too,« I answer, resigned, »but what's worse is really ...« I start anew.

»It must have been horrible for you, I see it. And you probably didn't eat properly, either. Now Harry will prepare a big plate of food for you. Food will soothe your nerves, and after you've finished, you'll tell me everything that happened.« She briefly pats me on the shoulder before disappearing into the kitchen to give her instructions.

Good old practical Grace.

I briefly consider calling Dan, but I quickly drop the idea. What could I tell him? »I'm scared, I feel threatened.« He would come and try to talk me into returning to Boston. There everything would be exactly the same way as when I left a few months ago. No, that would be the most unfavorable solution of all.

I walk over to the restaurant and sit down at our table next to the counter. From this place, which is somewhat concealed, I watch the other guests. As usually, most of the guests are in their thirties to late forties. Workers from the nearby paper mill or shipyard, who have a beer or a thick hamburger after work. They don't take notice of me; they're too immersed in their own conversations.

Grace puts a cup of hot tea in front of me.

»The food will be ready in a minute,« she says and sits down.

»I don't even know if I'm hungry,« I try to object.

»Your appetite will come with the food,« she brushes off my objection, changing the subject. »It's good to be among people again, right?«

I have to agree with her. In fact, I enjoy the murmur of voices and even the tobacco smoke that makes me feel safe today.

Shortly afterwards, when Harry places an appetizing plate in front of me with a juicy steak, fried potatoes and vegetables, I eat it with increasing pleasure, the whole plate empty. I even like the beer Grace brings me, even though I never drink beer otherwise.

A pleasant feeling of fatigue spreads through me. Now I can report the events a little more calmly. That doesn't make the story more credible, I know that. Grace doesn't say that, but she's trying hard to find a realistic reason for what happened.

»Karen, do you have an old admirer, one you once rejected? A former colleague from the last or an earlier publisher? Someone who knows you're in Maine now?«

I briefly go over the former colleagues and friends. No, with the best will in the world. Robert?

»No, there is no one I can imagine.«

Harry, who has cleared the empty plate with satisfaction, sits down with us. He feels complicit in my dilemma and feels he has to justify himself.

»I didn't tell him exactly where Karen lived, just about the direction. I also told him that it was impossible for someone unfamiliar with the location to find it. I advised him to meet her here.«

»Obviously he didn't want that,« I say. »He must have had reasons.«

»Maybe I shouldn't have given him an answer. Maybe I shouldn't have told him that Karen is with us regularly. Perhaps I should have pretended not to know her at all,« he continues in his self-accusations.

»It's okay,« Grace taps him on the shoulder soothingly. »You couldn't suspect anything bad. And strictly speaking, we don't even know if it is this person who is now sneaking around Karen's house. The story remains mysterious, no matter how we turn it, there is simply no reasonably obvious motive. Karen, you should stay here for a few days,« Grace suggests. She realizes how tired I've gotten. »You are definitely too much alone. Think about it.«

»It's not that I get along well with being alone,« I say to her. »But ...« I forego further fruitless explanations of something that obviously cannot be explained.

»I can no longer leave Leo alone. But today I'm happy if I can stay.«

20

Shortly afterwards I lie in one of the tiny guest rooms. When I put out the light, the confused pictures of the previous night come back to life. Was he in the house? Did he touch me? I grope along my body. It doesn't reveal anything. The wine! There must have been something in the wine, something that made me believe all the pictures, voices and sounds. I should never have drunk the wine. I have to pick up the bottle that was on the table yesterday and have it checked. Perhaps something can be ascertained from its content. Then at least I would have proof. Why didn't I take it with me?

It has become quiet in the pub. Every now and then the glimmer of light from a passing car scurries through the room. How different the sounds are. I enjoy the feeling of not being alone in the house, but under one roof with several people. What a tempting idea is it to stay here or maybe even go on to my parents in Michigan. It would be very easy. I could pick up Leo the next day and what I really need, maybe even together with Grace. Everything else sometime later.

But I can already hear the triumphant voices: »We knew it wouldn't work. We warned you. We never did understand why you would want to give up your relationship, the wonderful house and your wonderfully secure life. Karen, go back to Boston or Michigan.«

21

Everyone else knew what's best for me. Though I guess hardly anyone would believe what has happened in the last few weeks. They would think it was just my imagination. Even Grace didn't believe me. And one day I might even doubt it myself. I envision myself getting old in my parents' house and never again daring to take on new adventures.

No, I'm not going to run away. I will stay, find the explanation for the events and finish my book. Of course I have to protect myself, and I already have an idea. After making up my mind, I feel good. I'm calm inside. I bury myself in my pillows and am soon fast asleep.

I am awakened by unfamiliar sounds. It only surprises me to find out where I am. Voices and the smell of coffee penetrate my room. I get up and look out at the bright blue sky. There is already a lot of hustle and bustle on the road. After all, it is already ten a.m., I realize, astonished. After taking a short shower and quickly brushing my hair, I go downstairs.

Grace welcomes me; she looks pleased.

»Karen! You look a lot better today.«

»Yes, I slept like a log,« I confirm.

The breakfast table is already set. Milk, cornflakes and orange juice are waiting for me. Hash browns and fried egg are brought out of the kitchen, and Grace pours me a cup of coffee. Almost instantaneously I feel hungry. I haven't had a breakfast like this for ages.

»So how's your book doing? Have you been making good progress?«

»Yes, it'll be finished soon,« I answer absentmindedly. I have a very different question on my mind.

»Grace, do you have a gun?«

Grace doesn't miss the determination in my voice and looks up, startled. »What on Earth are you up to?«

»Relax. It's just in case. I don't expect I'll actually need it.«

»Well, there should be one around here somewhere. But I never used it myself. I don't even know if it still works.«

A few minutes later I hold a small, dainty metal object in my hand.

»Do you know how to handle it?« asks Grace.

»Not at all. I was hoping you'd ... «

Grace sighs and calls for Harry. His reaction is surprise, too.

»You want to hunt wolves now?« With childlike pleasure, he turns to the device that can kill a person and explains it to me with devotion. Grace watches us skeptically. Suddenly she gets up and returns a few moments later with a mobile phone.

»Take this in case there's an emergency – before you run the risk of shooting yourself. It's definitely easier to use.«

Gratefully I put both items into my pocket and get ready for the return trip. Outside it is dry and freezing cold.

»Take care of yourself,« Grace calls after me. »And if there's anything, call me or just come by!« She waves goodbye until I disappear behind a bend. In the supermarket I buy some groceries, and then I drive to the small hardware store on Pleasant Street. I urgently need security locks.

On the ride home I again have to concentrate on the road. Though it didn't snow last night, everything is frozen hard. I keep slipping and sliding on mirror-smooth surfaces, but the feeling of not being helpless any longer makes me feel courageous and strong. I will wait for him, set a trap for him. I will surprise him. I will beat him with his own weapons. The longer I drive, the more I talk myself into a battle mood. But maybe he won't even come back any more now that I've discovered him. He must be a coward; otherwise he wouldn't have run away.

When I arrive at the house, it's almost like the first time. The sun is shining, the sky is deep blue. A postcard landscape, frozen in frost. The house lies still and untouched, it seems abandoned and alien though I haven't been away for even twenty hours.

Uneasily I walk up to the front door, firmly clutching my purse. Thank God, at least the door is locked. Determined, I unlock it.

»Leo!« There is no trace of my cat, who usually welcomes me at the door. Where is he? Suddenly my throat constricts. I walk towards the kitchen and prepare for any kind of surprise. The room is tidy, wine bottle and petals have been removed. So he must have been in the house! Leo's food bowl is empty. But where is Leo? Did he let the cat out again? No, that's unlikely – Leo would have met me outside; he knows my car very well. »Leo!« I yell through the window nevertheless. Nothing moves in the bushes behind the house. There is also nothing unusual in the living room. By now I'm alarmed. My fear is turning into panic.

What did he come up with for me this time? Automatically I grope for the gun in my pocket. I feverishly try to remember Harry's instructions. I clutch the object with my trembling right hand. I clamp my purse under my left arm so I have it in case I have to run. Slowly I climb the stairs to my bedroom. As I enter the room, a piercing scream cuts through the silence. It takes me an eternity to realize that it is me who is screaming. Next to my bed, Leo is lying in a large pool of blood.

»Leo, Leo, Leo!« Sobbing, I sink to the ground, burying my face in his fur. He is still warm, but his heart is no longer beating. Leo, he was looking for me, my smell or even my help. And I wasn't there. Oh, my wonderful, tender friend, how loyal he was in the last few months! I remember the small, spirited fur ball Dan brought me one evening, and he was the only one who managed to warm me up. And I let him down. Tears run down my face. I stroke the lifeless animal with trembling hands. His joy when I woke up in the morning or when I came back to the house – as if he hadn't seen me for weeks. His cheerfulness when he returned from his forays. No more, never again! His anxiousness the day before yesterday when he ran towards me and trusted me to protect him. And then I left him alone and surrendered him to a monster. I caress Leo's tiny nose with the velvet coating I loved so much. His ears that no longer twitch, that used to react to the slightest noise even while he was sleeping fast. His beautifully colored head with his rigid, half-opened eyes is lying in my hand. He will never again cheerfully come running up to me or beg for food. How on Earth can I live on without you?

A sound startles me. Someone is at the front door, opening it. I'm paralyzed with fear. My sobbing subsides. I hear steps. Automatically I pick up the gun and get up. The intruder is coming upstairs. The gun in my hand trembles. I hold it with both hands. My pulse is hammering and racing. He's really come! I walk towards the stairs. My fingers clasp the gun. I search for the trigger, find it with my index finger. This is not a mystery thriller – this is real! The dark figure is approaching me step by step, stair by stair. »Stop!« I try to scream. My voice just makes a croaking sound. Unwavering, the massive figure comes closer. I don't have an escape route! He has almost reached the top of the staircase. Now I can see him. A shot is fired ...

»Nooooooo!« The Earth has stopped spinning.

Then a dull thud. It's not me; I'm still standing, I'm still alive. He is lying at the bottom of the staircase, moaning, reaching into the air with his hand. One last breath makes his heavy body shudder. Then everything is silent. His woolen cap has dropped. From above, I stare into a gray face, at beard stubbles, into blue eyes that are wide open, reflecting horror.

It can't be true! I crumble and drop to the ground. After a while I crawl to my purse and fumble for the phone.

»Grace, I just shot Dan.«

»*What?*« Her voice squeals into my ear. There is a short silence. »Stay where you are! I'll be right over!«

22

I am more exhausted than I have ever been in my whole life. I just want to lie down, think of nothing, just sleep. But as if I was petrified, I stay next to Leo. My hand keeps caressing his fur as if to comfort him. In fact, I'm comforting myself. It is completely quiet in the house; an odd sense of strangeness has come over me. Time stands still.

At some point I hear a car engine, male voices. Car doors slammed shut. They're coming. Steps sound in the house. Now they have reached him. Someone is coming upstairs. I will be handcuffed. But it's only Grace, who bends down to me.

Another person enters the room. »Are you hurt?«

»Me? Why? No.« Grace helps me get up and leads me to my bed.

»Grace, I didn't want that,« I whimper.

»I know, Karen, I know. You've done the right thing. Everything will be okay,« she says to me as if I were a little child.

Suddenly the room has filled up with people. Questions rain down on me.

»Do you know the man? Did you have an argument? Did he threaten you?«

»Don't you see she's in shock?« Grace says.

Someone feels my pulse. I get an injection. »You'll calm down in a moment,« says a soothing male voice.

Someone drapes a jacket over my shoulders. »Can you walk?« Without resisting, I let myself be led towards the staircase. At the top of the stairs, I stop abruptly.

»No, don't worry,« Grace whispers, »they've already taken him away.«

Now they'll put me in jail, just like Sarah, I think.

A wave swept over me, pulled me away, took my breath away. I thought I would be smashed by a rock, but there was no impact. I sailed through empty space, without any support, infinitely, found myself in Michigan at some point, back at my parents' house. A boomerang, which had flown around the world, had returned to its starting point. Death or birth? I thought this was the end of me, but I survived. The police didn't want to know much from me. They only asked me a few questions, and then I could leave. For days I was stunned; then a merciful emptiness followed.

Yes, it is this particular cold that I remember when I think of that time. The frost of those days surrounded me even in heated rooms. I was hiding, was afraid of looks, I was afraid of gossip behind my back. I was free yet trapped. I didn't read any newspaper, I didn't watch TV, I didn't listen to the radio. I didn't want to know what was happening outside. In the past, horrible things had happened to other people, but now they had happened to me.

The letter burst into my shielded world like a bomb. The letter sounded objective and neutral. »To clarify some final questions, we would like to ask you to contact Lieutenant Harper at 3 p.m. on December 8 at the Boston Police Department, Room 227.«

What did they need me for? What was missing for them to close the case? I recalled some scraps of words, the mentioning of a letter. Long-forgotten remarks came back to my mind, changing their meaning by the hour.

Rita picked me up at the airport. I recognized her immediately in the waiting crowd though she looked different. She was wearing a burgundy red coat that I didn't know yet. Her hair was shorter; she looked older. Elegant and strangely alien. Her perfume was also new as I noticed during our brief embrace.

We didn't talk much as she steered the car through lunchtime traffic. A dark gray sky hung over the city. Dirty snow piled up on the side of the road. People rushed by like shadows.

»I won't stay in the city much longer,« Rita suddenly interrupted the silence.

»You? What are you planning to do?«

»I applied for a job with a newspaper in Los Angeles. I've had enough of those bleak winters. I got the word the day before yesterday.«

So now Rita, too. For a moment, her words had torn me away from my own thoughts. Will Robert go with her? I wondered. But I didn't ask.

The lieutenant seemed pleasant. After he had asked me to sit down across from him, however, he seemed to have forgotten me. He focused on the stack of documents in front of him, read some and leafed through them. At last he seemed to have found what he was looking for.

»Well,« he began thoughtfully, »I can confirm that your statements are essentially consistent with what we have found. There was a loaded gun in the hand of the deceased. There are also other factors that suggest that he intended a homicide. You acted in self-defense. If you hadn't fired your weapon, you wouldn't be sitting here today.«

Although his words confirmed my innocence and meant freedom to me, they hit home. Up to this hour I had firmly believed in the interaction of unhappy circumstances. I had been sure that Dan wanted to visit me because he cared about me, and that the madman who had threatened me for weeks was still somewhere out there.

I groaned.

»The facts are cut and dry. They don't allow for any other conclusion.« Harper had moved to an official tone. »We found an SUV near the crime scene, similar to the vehicle you had seen. It turned out that it had been rented by the deceased. Inside the car we found maps of Maine, as well as the following items« — he read from a list — »A key to a log cabin nearby the cottage. He must have stayed there for the last few weeks. A camera, two empty wine bottles containing residue of drugs. In the jacket of the deceased they found the included piece of jewelry and the car keys.«

He let the contents of a paper bag slide onto the table in front of me. It was the white gold chain with the aquamarine heart framed in diamonds. Dan's last gift. The lieutenant spread out some photos in front of me, photos of my beach cottage. One picture showed me walking along the shore on a stormy day.

»In the safe of his Boston home we found a wax print of the key to the beach house and documents concerning the fact that he had hired a detective to find the location of your house. We also found a will that had been written a few days earlier.«

»A will? Why should Dan want to make a will?«

Harper ignored my remark. »Who do you think he might have favored in his will?«

»I have no idea.« Fear rose in me.

The next question thundered down on me. »What do you know about your partner's family?«

»Not much, his parents are dead. He had no contact with other family members.«

»Is that what he told you?«

»Yes.«

»Does the name Susan Fernandez sound familiar?«

»No, who's that?« Tears shot into my eyes. His questions frightened me. I didn't understand any of this. »That's your partner's mother.«

It was suddenly quiet in the room. Then paper rattled. Harper handed me a letter. When I recognized the handwriting, my throat felt constricted. The letters blurred in front of my eyes.

Dear Mother,
once again I have to cause you sorrow, but maybe it will also be a relief for you. Believe me, I don't want to do it, but I can't bear another separation. I will go with the woman I love to where there is no return.

Maybe the house will make up for every sorrow I have caused you and am causing again. It shall be yours. I can imagine that you will like it. You have always loved beautiful things so much. The money in the account is for grandmother. I know I have never thanked her enough for her care. I couldn't forgive her for talking badly about you. Presumably she meant well with me. I think everything would have turned out differently if I had lived with you. Karen is the woman I wanted to live with. If she had returned to me, none of this would have happened. Her return would have healed the wounds of the past. But this kind of happiness does not seem to be meant for me. Now, at least, death will unite us forever.
Forgive me, Your Loving Son
Dan

It was Dan's stationery, Dan's handwriting and Dan's signature. Dan had planned our two deaths with precision. I felt sick to my stomach. The lieutenant didn't seem to notice.

23

»Mrs. Fernandez didn't know where her son lived.«

»Why?« I asked, stunned.

»Oh, his family can explain this better to you.« I thought my heart would stop.

A few moments later she stood in front of me, with curiosity and a thousand questions in her eyes. She was blond and had his blue eyes. It was as if Dan was looking at me. I shuddered. I fearfully anticipated accusations, but Susan welcomed me with kindness.

»My mother was very beautiful,« Dan had once said. And Susan Fernandez *was* beautiful and incredibly young. She might as well have been his older sister.

»Karen, I'm so sorry. If only he had sent the letter earlier.«

Did she feel guilty? She was his mother.

»Your son was such a lonely person; why didn't you stay in touch with him?« That was the question that moved me the most.

Susan hesitated. »He didn't want to. One day he just disappeared from our lives without saying a word.«

»But why? He missed his family very much.«

Susan looked at me in silence for a moment. Then tears welled up in her eyes.

»Dan had been in jail, maybe that's why. Maybe he was ashamed of that. Perhaps this way he hoped to forget everything, to start anew.«

»Dan was in jail?« Everything in me rebelled against that idea. Susan, too, struggled before she continued. »He almost killed a woman once.«

Emptiness in my brain. My knees felt like they would buckle any second. Susan's hand touched me.

»That is why I was so worried when I received the letter.«

Dan, my dear, friendly Dan! I didn't want to believe it.

Then I remembered those horrible minutes on my last visit, when he had attacked and almost raped me. I remembered how afraid I had been of him then.

»Dan was extremely jealous,« Susan told me. »He wanted to possess his women. No, not just women. He wanted to possess everything that meant a lot to him.«

»Susan, that's too much at the moment. I don't think you should try to explain everything to her all at once.« The man who had stayed in the background until now intercepted lovingly and delicately.

»This is my husband,« Susan introduced Julio Fernandez to me. He was tall and slim and his hair was jet-black. He was quite handsome. Both of them were elegantly dressed. They made a beautiful couple. »You have always loved beautiful things so much«, Dan had written. Dan, too, had always been well-dressed; he had loved precious things, valuable paintings, expensive carpets, fine porcelain. In this, mother and son were alike.

»Julio is Dan's stepfather. Dan never met his biological father. We were both very young.«

Susan had been fifteen when Dan was born. Just a child. She still looked so young.

»I wanted him to be happy with his own family,« she said. She talked a lot. She talked about him, trying to explain, asking questions and imploring. »Everything could've been so wonderful, so good for everyone if only ...«

24

They wanted to go see the house, taking me with them to his house. After all, I still had some of my things there, and I could tell them so much about the last few years with Dan. And they could tell me about the years before that.

»We haven't heard from him for eight years.«

I was shocked and embarrassed about thinking that they just wanted to see his house, their heritage, as soon as possible. Then I understood the tension behind Susan's flood of words. I had killed her son, and yet she was clinging to me. I was the last woman he had lived with. I was the only part of her son she had left. Me and his house.

They told me that Dan's grandmother was waiting for them in a rental car nearby. She had wanted to accompany them, not to the police but to the city, to the house where Dan had last lived.

»Dan grew up with her; he was her favorite, her whole life. It's especially hard for her.«

As we drove to the house on Beacon Street, I told Rita, who had been waiting outside, what had happened in the last hour. The Fernandez' blue rental car followed us. The short ride was only long enough for a rough description of the results. Then we arrived at the parking lot. Susan was a little familiar to me now, in contrast to the old woman who struggled to get out of the car. How different the two women were. I wouldn't have thought that they were mother and daughter.

»Mother, that's Karen. She lived with Dan.«

The old woman did not offer me her hand; she just nodded curtly. Her eyes reflected resignation. Her skin was wrinkled, her eyes reddened. I felt rejected. I felt hit by small sharp arrows from narrow eye slits. Glowing lava in a withering body. She had loved him. He had been young and handsome and well-educated. She was old and simple. She had lived for him.

Dan had not loved his grandmother. Dan had loved what he couldn't get. The less he had been loved, the more he had loved. He had once told me that he had grown up with an aunt, a loveless, strict aunt.

Residue of the seal still stuck to the door. I felt fear, terrible fear. My hands trembled when I put the key in the lock.

My eyes fell on a bouquet of roses. It was the bouquet that Dan had given me on my last visit. Now the flowers were even darker, almost black. I couldn't take my eyes off them. They reminded me of another bouquet of roses. They had sat on the table in the beach house and also been nearly black. Black and soft, velvety to the touch. The memory sent shivers down my spine. These petals here were dry and rustled like paper.

The others had quietly entered the house behind me. They were impressed and visibly surprised.

»What an exquisite home,« Susan whispered. »Did Dan furnish it or did you?«

»Dan did it. He renovated and furnished the house. That was before we met. Please feel free to look around.« Without caring about what the others were doing, I walked on. I was shocked by what I saw. There were glasses and bottles scattered throughout the living room and kitchen, everything was dusty. All the plants were dead. Dan had always been so neat. I recalled a different face. The pale face with the empty eyes and the unkempt beard stubbles.

»We couldn't get in touch with Dan in the last weeks,« Rita told me. »We thought he had gone to join you in Maine.«

»That's probably what he did,« I remarked bitterly, »only I knew nothing about it.«

»Karen, he didn't let anyone get close to him anymore. He had even sent his cleaning lady away. He hadn't gone to work for a long time either. Nobody had any idea how serious things were.« Rita seemed deeply shocked.

Glasses and bottles were in every room, too. I could hear murmurs in the hallway. The things they must be thinking! But then I heard exclamations of admiration.

»Look at that painting and these magnificent carpets!" Susan said excitedly.

»Dan wasn't a bad boy and he was so smart,« I heard his grandmother say.

»Yes, mother, no one says he wasn't. But he was always difficult, since I can remember. You have to admit that.«

»You should have taken better care of him, Susan. Dan needed you.«

»If you hadn't spoiled him so much, it would have been easier for everyone.«

»Now it's supposed to be *my* fault!« The old lady's voice sounded outraged. »There's no point in blaming each other,« I heard Julio Fernandez say.

In the living room I suddenly had to think of Halloween, of our last time together. Of the meal Dan and Rita had prepared together, of Robert's kiss, his declaration of love, which had made me tremble. Of Dan's brutal assault, which I had perceived as rape. Had my rejection ignited the disastrous events that were to follow?

Was that when it happened? At breakfast the next morning he had seemed so gentle, so conciliatory, even as we were strolling past all these witches and ghosts to the Margarita restaurant, where it had all begun. Maybe it hadn't happened until the evening of that day. Dan had been so silent. Was the plan born while I was lying in bed, sleeping tight because of the sleeping pills I had taken, relieved to be able to return to Maine in the morning? Was that when he made the wax print of the key to the beach cottage? Now I was sure of it.

»He achieved so much, he could have been happy,« I heard Susan's voice from the stairwell.

»Dan wanted to be loved«, answered an old, trembling voice. »Mother, it was never enough for him.«

In Dan's study, a picture hung from the wall. The safe was open now. Empty. This was where the police had found the documents documenting the diligent preparation of the project. Had he kept his pistol here? How long had he already had it?

The blankets of both beds in the bedroom were disheveled. There were more bottles and glasses standing around in this room. Disgusted, I put my clothes into suitcases. Rita, who had followed me to the bedroom, helped me. We packed my things in silence.

When everything was packed, I climbed the stairs to the attic one last time. By myself. My former study looked untouched. Apparently nobody had entered it since I had last left it. Once again, I looked over the gloomy gray city. It was an exact mirror of my state of mind.

When I had entered the house, everything had reminded me of the man I had once known and loved. When I left the house, he was a stranger to me.

Rita drove me to the airport. A quick farewell, just a few words. A fleeting hug, a thoughtful look.

»Take care, Karen.« She turned and rushed away. Rita, my cheerful friend, who was often incredibly naive and lowbrow, had fallen silent. We had both changed.

25

What followed was a Christmas filled with painful memories.

A year ago I had celebrated Christmas with Dan and my family. My father had proudly given him a tour of his company. Dan seemed to enjoy family life. Grief would alter with anger. How much he had lied to me from the start!

Not long after that Dan appeared in my dream. Tears streamed down my face and made me tremble. I shouted at him, »What have you done? You wanted to kill me?«

Dan was silent, his gaze was sad. He left as he had come.

But he came again, in a very different dream. He entered my room wordlessly and placed a basket full of colorful primroses on my desk. He looked at me imploringly before he left.

The pain changed; it was no longer a sharp, burning pain but rather a soft pain full of wistfulness. Soon there was something tender, almost touching about it. The battle was over. I felt tired.

March. The first spring sun made the snow melt. Around noon, the dark soil started to steam and spread an earthy smell. The sight reminded me of a grave, but new life grew on it. Weeds, a delicate new green. Essential things meet at one point. Yes and no, beginning and end, day and night, black and white. Today exists only because of yesterday. I often wondered if perhaps I should have gone to Salem? Then I wouldn't have met Rita nor my work colleague, whom I fell in love with – unhappily. The sudden separation from him was the reason for my move to Globus. There I met Dan.

Did I have a choice? Every single puzzle piece was part of my life. Only all of them together created an overall picture. Everything falls into place. Once again, it was grandmother who was good for me, and simple physical work. Together we worked in her backyard next to the house. Digging in the dark soil, sowing and planting kept me from digging in my memories. Exercise and fresh air healed my body and my soul. In the midst of this healing process, the past caught up with me. It was Sarah who appeared in my dream. She was sitting in her cell, and her blue eyes looked at me reproachfully. »Did you forget about me?« she asked. »Do you think you can start a new life before you finish our story?«

That dream haunted me. I kept thinking about it for days. I knew Sarah was right. I, on the other hand, was afraid to deal with the story. I was afraid of the memories that were associated with her. Did I really have to go through the whole thing again?

»I'm thinking about finishing my book,« I said one day while my grandmother and I looked at the first delicate leaves of the plants we had sown not long ago.

»A great idea,« said grandmother, surprised and delighted. It wasn't until that moment that I knew I was really going to do it. A few hours later, I summoned up the courage to approach the boxes that had been sitting untouched in the corner of my room for months. I opened them, took my computer and printer out, arranged everything on the desk. I turned on the computer and searched excitedly for the file. The text, I hope I'll find the backed-up text. I remembered having hidden the floppy disk in the closet. Another one should be in a floppy disk box. Oh my God, where did they go? I rummaged between sweaters and kitchen utensils and finally had to unpack everything. A thousand memories fluttered up like black ravens, sat down on the table and bed and soon filled the whole room. In the midst of this chaos I discovered the small black plastic square in one of the pockets of my winter jacket. I pushed the floppy disk into the drive. Miraculously, it had survived all the turbulences intact. After a few moments, the manuscript was back on the hard drive and seconds later on my screen. Impatiently, I printed everything out and started reading. The longer I read, the more I realized I had nothing to fear. I saw blue skies, Sarah and Tom as a carefree couple, seagulls roaring through the air, I heard the sound of the ocean, the seagulls and voices. I remembered the storms in autumn, the wet cold of the winter by the sea and the crackling of the fire in the beach house. But most of all, I realized that the story captivated me; though some places made me sad, they didn't scare me anymore. Again and again I read the last lines; then I saw Sarah leaving the prison. In slow motion, she stepped out of the darkness into daylight. She was blinded by the light. Sarah smiled at me. The end of my novel unfolded before me. All I had to do now was write it down.

Sarah has calmed down. Her feelings of despair and her sudden rage have become rarer and eventually disappeared altogether. She has learned to fight in a different way. She uses her energy more sparingly. Almost relaxed, she awaits the next day of her trial. Her stomach revolts only briefly on the way to the courtroom. She enters the room quietly, holding her chin up. She feels at once that this time everything is different. There is a completely different atmosphere. The courtroom is crowded with many Western trial observers. A representative of the American consulate is present. There is hardly any room for sensation mongers. When the trial begins, she feels the eyes of the people looking at her with open sympathy. And now she understands Hamid, too. No, today he isn't emphatic and soft either, but now she knows that he is fighting for her. Tough, emotionless, cool, matter-of-fact. He knows exactly what he is doing. The customs officials seem nervous; they no longer agree with each other and entangle themselves in contradictions. Hamid ruthlessly tightens the noose. The presence of the foreign press makes the parties more cautious. Everyone is trying to act properly. A machine has been set in motion, late, but effective. The media are mobilized. The Western newspapers and every news program report about Sarah's case. Tourism seems to be at risk, especially when it is revealed that Sarah has never been involved with drugs before.

Witnesses have been summoned to appear today. At last, Mitchell comes into play. Passengers on that fateful flight testify. They report their observations in regards to Mitchell's activities. They confirm his suspicious behavior. The man who was to heal her from the pain of love has plunged her into a much deeper disaster. The others had long since sensed what he was up to.

Sighs, relief, murmuring voices; they sound like applause. Flashlights. Sarah knows she has won.

I quickly stepped back into the story, and I enjoyed writing it down. It hadn't all been in vain. I would finish writing the book, and everything would be alright. Knowing this gave me a great sense of satisfaction.

Outside, spring was pulsating. The trees had exploded in a beautiful wealth of blossoms; birds were singing. I thought of my two dreams. Cold turned into heat. Snow turned into petals. The storm had become a spring song. Window bars just dissolved, and in the blue spring sky, seagulls drew their tracks, cheering. Can dreams sometimes become true after all?

26

It became summer, and the plants grew quickly in their vegetable patches. Grandmother and I tried to control the wildly sprouting weeds. The sun was burning down on our heads. We sweated profusely.

»I think we should take a break,« Grandmother suggested and disappeared into the house to make coffee. I straightened up to give my aching back a break and wiped my forehead. A strand of hair had escaped the barrette I was wearing. That was the moment I saw him. He came walking straight at me. At first I didn't see it; the sun blinded me too much. His face looked almost black in the backlight. But his movements, so calm and powerful! That can't be possible! My knees started to buckle. My fingers grasped the hoe. He was so beautiful. Oh, that adorable smile, these blackish brown eyes.

»Robert! What are you doing here?«

He didn't answer but just wrapped his arms around me. I felt the warmth of his body on my face. That fragrance! I leaned against him with closed eyes.

»I love you. I love you so much. I missed you so much.« His voice sounded warm and infinitely tender. It hit me right in the heart. I felt dizzy. A wave of happiness lifted me off the ground. For a tiny, wonderful eternity, I thought I was floating. How good it was to feel his violently pounding heart.

»You are so beautiful.«

He shouldn't have said that.

»My God, how do I look?« I was sweating, wearing my oldest shorts, probably had soil on my face. It was like when I first saw him. In a matter of seconds I had turned into a gray mouse. The memory sobered me up. I broke away from him. »Robert ... where's Rita?«

»Probably in Los Angeles.«

»But ...«

»It's over.«

»Why?«

»You know why.«

»No, I don't.«

»You don't? It was right after that.«

»Right after what?«

»After I had kissed you.«

Oh my God, was that why Rita had changed so much?

»Does she know?«

»It hadn't been the way it used to be for a long time. Did she know that I love you? I don't know, maybe she guessed it. Yes, she probably guessed it.«

»I didn't want that to happen.«

»No one is to blame, Karen. Love is not a crime.«

»Nein, es geht nicht Robert, es geht nicht!« Ich schob ihn ein Stück von mir weg. Robert redete auf mich ein. Während er mich beschwor, fühlte ich eine gläserne Wand zwischen uns. Er schien sie auch zu spüren. Trotz der Sonne hatte sich alles verfinstert. Robert versuchte mir etwas zu erklären.

»Ich liebe dich. Verstehst du mich nicht.«

Ich trat einen Schritt zurück.

»Es geht nicht Robert. Es ist zu viel geschehen.« Hilflos zuckte ich mit den Schultern.

»Karen, du kannst wieder glücklich werden, wenn du es nur willst.«

Nochmals versuchte er, mich in den Arm zu nehmen. Erneut wich ich aus. Er griff ins Leere. Enttäuscht ließ er seine Arme sinken. Then he took a notepad out of his chest pocket, scribbled something on a piece of paper, ripped it off and pressed it into my hand.

»Maybe one day you will think differently about it.«

He turned around and left.

I was crying. I want it to stop, I thought. I want to forget everything. I want to work in the yard, write my book and stop thinking about it. I don't want to be reminded of it.

»Has your visitor left already?« Grandmother, who had returned to the garden, asked.

I hadn't noticed her.

»Why, have you seen him?«

»Of course. I sent him into the yard.« She carried a tray of coffee and cups and looked at me, worried. »Come, let's sit down; then it's easier to talk.«

I took the tray from her and carried it to the gazebo.

»Did he have bad news for you?« she asked after pouring the coffee into the cups.

»He said he loves me.«

»And?«

»Grandmother, he was with my best friend until recently.«

»But now they are separated?«

»Yes.«

She looked at me inquiringly. »Do you love him?«

»Maybe. I don't know; there was a time when I believed I did.«

»What's the problem?«

»I think he's a philanderer.«

»You think so? He seems to be very nice and is very good-looking.« She peered at me from the side, looking impish.

»Yes, he's handsome and charming. And I think he knows it, too.«

»You think he's playing with women?«

»In any case, his job involves a lot of traveling, and so he certainly has lots of opportunities.«

»Oh, Karen, nobody can guarantee you happiness and fidelity. You know that. But at least give him and happiness a chance.«

»Would you start a relationship with a man like him?«

»My child, in my days we couldn't have relationships. We married our men and then got to know them.«

»But you were happy in your marriages?«

»The first one, I'm not sure; maybe it could have been happy. We didn't have enough time to find out. But of course, when my first husband died, I thought my life was over. The truth is, I didn't know much about life back then.«

»And then Grandpa Paul came along?«

»Yes, then Paul came along, and you know what? He used to be the greatest ladies' man in town.«

»Grandpa Paul a ladies' man?« I didn't want to believe what I was hearing.

Grandmother smiled with amusement. »Everybody warned me about him. I dared to marry him anyway — and have never regretted it even for a moment. I'm glad I listened to my heart.«

»Weren't you worried?« I asked, horrified, unable to picture my dear Grandpa Paul in the role of a lady killer and heartbreaker.

»But of course, child, very much, but what was the alternative? A dreary widowhood or an even drearier married life with one of the bores that wanted to marry me, too. I gave Paul and us a chance.«

»Was that very difficult, at the beginning, I mean? Was Grandpa Paul faithful to you?«

»Yes, he was faithful. Of course, as in any marriage, there were some stormy times. But not a single day with him was boring, not to this day.« As she said so, her eyes shone like those of a young girl. »Honestly, turbulence and a bit of adventure are part of life. They are the salt in the soup. Some need a little less, others need a little more of it. It is the powerful, active people who move the world. By the way, there were several in our family. If it hadn't been for them, we wouldn't be here now. Maybe we wouldn't even exist. Do you remember the crazy stories about Uncle Norman, who traveled all over the world in the most adventurous ways, at a time when that was by no means a common thing to do?«

»Is this the man in the safari suit with the slain tiger at his feet?«

»Yes, how do you know the picture?«

»It was in a cardboard box full of photos in your attic.« Grandmother's eyes light up.

»Actually, I had completely forgotten them.« She quickly disappeared and came back a short time later with the box. We sat over a mountain of yellowed photos until dusk. I learned the sad story of Great-grandmother Helen, whose husband died while traveling from Ireland to America with her two children. She entered the country, where had she wanted to start a new, better life with him, as a widow. Brave and courageous, she had taken her fate into her own hands and made it. My mother's ancestors are said to be from France ... And there was ...

»And these are just the ones we know. There are many more of whom we know nothing, and yet you carry something in you from all of them.« I saw legions of ancestors before me.

»Maybe some from Italy, from Rome,« I whispered quietly to myself.

»Maybe, who knows?« Grandmother agreed. Her mind was in a different time, a different world.

For the first time ever I consciously looked at my grandmother. How beautiful she was, so youthful and vibrant. In her serenity, she resembled Grace. But she was happier and more temperate. Oh, how I loved this humorous, brave little woman in that moment.

27

Hesitantly Sarah steps out into freedom. It is very different from what she imagined, much less spectacular yet overwhelming. There is so much space, so much light, there are so many sounds and voices. The six months in prison were endless — and short at the same time. She is now a different woman from the one who entered prison at the time. Tom comes to meet her, he holds a bouquet in his hand, small pastel pink roses. Her favorite flowers. He smiles, but his smile seems artificial. His embrace is a little stiff and hesitant, too. Then he takes her bag with her few possessions and leads her to the cab.

»I booked a suite at the Regent Hotel for us,« he says and tells the cabdriver the address. »I figured that after the last few months you went through you deserve some luxury. Besides, you don't want to be immediately attacked by journalists and colleagues.«

Strangely, Sarah had never thought about what she would do immediately after being released from jail. She had always thought only of the moment when she would step through the door into the open. When she had thought of freedom, she had thought about things like being free per se. Being able to go wherever she wanted. Sleeping, eating, taking a shower whenever she wanted to. Deciding herself whether she wanted to be by herself or with other people. And slipping under fresh, fragrant covers at night. She had not pictured *where* her bed would be. Nor how she would meet Tom. Actually she had hardly ever thought of him any more. Though she had never doubted it that he would pick her up, just like he had provided her with a lawyer and fulfilled her modest wishes. He was just there, no less, no more.

Sarah enters the posh hotel lobby with Tom. Will everyone be able to tell where she comes from just by looking at her? No one seems to be paying attention to her. She feels relieved when she has reached the suite on one of the upper floors.

It consists of two large, luxuriously furnished rooms and an exquisite bathroom. The splendor overwhelms her yet she doesn't feel true happiness. Somewhat helplessly, Sarah looks around. My God, how big everything is.

The windows provide a dreamlike view over the city. Tom is irritated by her silence.

»Sarah, don't you like it?«

»Of course I do; it's beautiful.« At that moment she realizes that she hasn't really missed this kind of luxury. She remembers her imagined trips, which meant freedom to her during the time of imprisonment. They were excursions to fields lush with summer flowers, to shady forests that smelled of spicy evergreens and to peaceful beaches at sunset.

There is a knock on the door. Sarah winces. It's a waiter who serves a cooler with champagne and two glasses. After he's gone, Tom fills the glasses.

»Cheers, Sarah!«

The champagne is cold and sparkling. Sarah feels how the cool liquid fills her mouth and then flows through her esophagus, enters her blood circulation and spreads through her whole body. She starts to feel pleasantly dizzy. The world begins to revolve around her, and suddenly Sarah finds everything hilariously funny.

»I think I'm getting tipsy. They didn't serve any alcohol at the hotel where I stayed last.«

»Are you hungry? Maybe we should eat something?«

»Yes, I think I'm going to eat everything on the menu from top to bottom today. But first I want to take a long hot bath.«

»Do everything you feel like. I brought some of your clothes.«

The bathroom is huge. Everything is so great but feels so unreal. Sarah feels like on a movie set. She lets the bathtub fill up with water while she undresses. Then she examines herself in the large crystal mirror that extends over the entire width of the room. How narrow her face and body have become! Her skin shimmers very pale; her eyes look huge. She almost forgot what she looks like. Her body had become alien to her, she had barely noticed it anymore. She has to learn to feel it again. Actually she has to learn a lot of things anew; she can't take anything for granted anymore.

Sarah emerges in a sea full of wonderfully fragrant foam. She closes her eyes, enjoys the warm water that is gently moving around her, and sinks into a soothing infinity.

»Sarah, are you fine, is everything okay?«Tom's voice sounds concerned.

»Yes, yes, I'll be out in a minute.«

She lathers her body with soap, rinses the soap off with cool water and climbs out of the tub. Then she wraps one of the fluffy towels around her body and dries her hair with a blow-dryer. Finally she slips into one of the dresses Tom brought along. It hangs loosely from her body. She tries another one; it doesn't fit any better either. This fashion show seems ridiculous to her. She finds a lipstick in her purse and paints her lips a delicate pink shade. Since she has no other make-up, she also uses it as blusher. At least she looks a bit refreshed now. Tom awaits her with an expectant look on his face.

»I'm afraid I have nothing fancy I can wear to the diningroom of this place. So I think we'll have to eat in this room.«

»There's a boutique downstairs. I could get you something. I'm sure they'll give me a selection of clothes for you to choose from. They also have evening dresses. Sarah, you would probably look stunning in one of those.«

»No, I have neither any jewelry nor any make-up with me.«

»There's a jewelry shop and a drugstore downstairs, too.«

Sarah looks at him thoughtfully.

»I'm happy to get you everything you need.«

Is Tom perhaps afraid of being alone with her? She looks at him with determination. »No, I think I'd rather eat here. My company has to be enough for you.«

»I just thought you wanted ... after everything ...«

»I want to eat in this room, in my clothes. I don't want to dress up, and your company is enough for me.«

»Okay, Sarah, it's your day.« Tom gives in.

Yes, today he will do anything she wants. Anything? Sarah briefly feels a small triumph. As she flips through the menu, she suddenly craves food. The wealth of dishes makes her mouth water. She orders a starter, a main dish and dessert. Not much later the food is served. They eat more or less in silence. Sarah is full much faster than her appetite made her believe.

»What is it, Sarah? Don't you like it?«

»My appetite was bigger than my stomach. I can't eat that much anymore.«

Tom anxiously tries to cater to her every need. He looks at her uncertainly.

Will he do everything she asks for now? Will he love her if she wants him to? Can she have him back?

»How is Shirley?«

Tom blushes.

»She's fine. She is very relieved that everything went so well for you. Yeah, yeah, I know, but she really felt miserable about what happened. Honestly, Sarah, even if you can't believe it.«

Sarah looks at him seriously.

»All right, Tom, I don't see Shirley as my rival anymore. The world, life is not what it was a few months ago. Tom, I'm free and I will start over. And you, Tom ... you're free, too.«

»Sarah ...«

»I think Shirley is a good match for you. I will fly home and start over, do something new. Maybe even study again, law or medicine.«

Tom exhales noticeably.

It is their last night together, filled with conversations about a past that is just ending, and a future that is beginning at the same time. At some point they fall asleep on the comfortable wide seating. The luxurious bed remains untouched.

Shirley looks at Tom anxiously and expectantly. He walks up to her quickly, hugs her, whispers something into her ear. Her eyes brighten up. She laughs, she beams. They go to the beach, where they fool around. A young couple, happy and carefree, as if the months before had not happened. They remind me of another couple, of a couple an eternity ago.

I see a new image. Shirley and Tom stroll through a city with old houses and narrow streets. They enter small stores. Shirley slips into colorful clothes. Tom puts a necklace around her neck and they try on some rings. He takes pictures of her. Shirley poses for him. She is tanned and her eyes shine tenderly. It is an old but a very lively city. They are in Rome. Roman Forum, Coliseum, Basilica Aemilia, Via Appia. Interesting pictures. Cappuccino, tagliatelle, Bardolino, Chianti. Shirley struggles with the longest spaghetti she ever had. Tom tries to show her how to handle them better. They are surrounded by music. They dance until the early hours of the morning, staggering drunk with love over the Spanish Stairs, counting the steps that lead steeply up to heaven, to happiness.

Everything starts again. The drama has become a crime novel and, at the end of the day, a love story. The circle has closed. The day, the game, the year, the love.

I'm with them in Rome. I lose myself in the pictures. Fontana di Trevi. Shirley throws coins into it. There were three. Three coins will result in eternal love, someone once told me. Who was it? A sense of yearning flares up in me. I fill the beautiful pictures with ever more details. Quirinal, Esquilin, Pincio, Gianicolo, the eternal city at my feet.

I get up abruptly. I'm looking for a note. It's a note with a phone number scribbled on it. Excited, I search through my clothes. I find it, small and wrinkled, in my shorts. The numbers are hardly legible anymore. Hopefully the number is still the right one. I dial them with trembling fingers. It seems to take forever. Then finally his voice answers the phone.

»Robert, will you fly to Rome with me?«

About the Author
Christine Brendle

The author, Christine Brendle, wanted to spend one year in Maine after becoming a widow at the age of 30 with three young children. And not just to spend her vacation there, as she used to with her husband and children in the past, but to experience every season and daily life in New England.

Three years after the tragedy, she made her dream come true and it turned out to be the most important experience in her life. It has made her bolder. And the images of Maine found their way into her first novel.

The author was born in Austria, near Lake Constance. After reading her first book at the age of seven, she was hooked on literature. And she always wanted to go to America, especially after a neighbor of hers had gone to the U.S. because of an inheritance and returned with such precious objects as see-through high heels. It had to be a wonderful country, the child figured.

After her major dream – that of a happy family – was shattered, she remembered her other dreams – still or even more now: America and literature. In the years after her stay in Maine, she became an author and later a publisher. It only made sense to combine her dreams into a novel.

The result is a romantic mystery story filled with adventures that tells of fear and courage, of longing and insecurities and of dreams that are greater and more powerful than any doubts.

Thank to Carolyn Murphey-Melchers

»Thank you, Carolyn, for your wonderful proofreading and final suggestions.«